20 CENTIMOS PALMAS

MW01274201

POR VIA AEREA

13.FEB 37

LAS PALMAS

FRANQUICIA POSTAL
CORREOS
14 JULIO 1931
REPUBLICA ESPAÑOLA
CORTES CONSTITUYENTES

12   12

DEUTSCHES REICH

ESPAÑA

20 CTS

Alargalavida
www.alargalavida.es

Book: Elwinga's Watch
© **Texts:** Sandra Franco Álvarez and Juan José Monzón Gil
© **Illustrations:** Elena Ferrándiz
© **Cover design and page layout:** Álex Falcón
© **Photo of the writers:** Pepa Guerra

....

Editorial Bilenio - Editorial Stamp from LIJ Alargalavida
www.bilenio.com   www.alargalavida.es

....

Second edition, May 2020
Las Palmas de Gran Canaria

....

Legal deposit: GC 272-2020
ISBN: 9798813646331

....

Font: Goudy Old Style, Garamond.

....

*"The ultimate tragedy is not the oppression and cruelty
by the bad people but the silence over that
by the good people."*

Martín Luther King

Prologue

I began to read the book with my mind but as I turned the pages, I began to feel it deep in my stomach.

Without realising, I had switched from "them" to "myself", and my heart was beating in the body of each character.

It's a story of stories, a fight for survival in body, soul and memory; of travels, uprooting and adventures.

This is a novel about ogres, or in other words, "the same ogre in a different collar". Phrases like "their names no longer exist" were decreed by the thousand tongues of the monster whose evil was so real that it now seems like fiction.

However, this watch does not want to turn back to that time of frightened boys, or girls waiting day in day out for the return of their parents who were grabbed by the ogre; the book's very heartbeat repairs their wounds to a certain extent. They didn't wait in vain.

This book gives us an all-powerful spear to fight with in the form of memory... because monsters feast on forgetting.

The voices of Sophie, Moshé and Josefina pass on their memories so that, no matter how many ways the darkness disguises its true face, we have the means to recognise it and beat it.

"Elwinga's Watch" contains treasures in the form of diaries, watches and even sea snails. The thread of its action is beautifully woven by violin and timple strings, making a knot in our throats and invisible threads that sew deep emotional bonds between different ages, places and cultures.

I also liked how the authors tackle the subject matter, never underestimating their young readers. They write smoothly, poetically, weaving in suspense and reality. And hope! So much hope! Amid the broken glass, they manage to grow real flowers in the form of acts of kindness, helping hands, and voices that provide shelter and consolation.

I would recommend this book to young people, schools and families, as a healing antidote so that young people can share their reading with their fathers, mothers, grandfathers, grandmothers, teachers and neighbours.

Because "Talking" and "Meeting" were verbs once prohibited by the ogre of darkness who was determined to inject people with the poison of fear and silence.

I honestly believe that every time someone reads "Elwinga's Watch" and shares it, the ogre dies a little bit more.

MARINA WAINER
March 2020

Elwinga's watch

Sandra Franco Álvarez
Juan José Monzón Gil

Translation by: Kit Cree

My name is Moshé Abramsky

Poland

I came into the world in 1924, born in the tough inter-war period.

My name is Moshé, son of Josek and Clara Abramsky. I was born in a town close to Lublin, lying east of the River Vistula, and lived there until I was eight years old.

Mama and Tata were thrilled by my arrival. They had been trying to have a baby for a long time and had accepted that it would never happen to them.

I had a happy childhood although I would always have liked a brother or sister to play with, especially during the endless winter days, when fierce winds and storms kept the schools closed.

I never met my grandparents, just an ageing aunt in the village, because the rest of my family, on both sides, had either emigrated or been called up to fight at the front. Tata had been luckier there - he was so short-sighted, his glasses so thick, that he narrowly escaped the Great War.

I grew up to be a bookworm, just like my father, and my mother taught me to play the violin and to cherish our rich Polish folklore. She often used to say that if I wanted to get the hang of the instrument one day, I'd first have to learn to dance mazurka and polonaise.

When my paternal grandparents died, Tata inherited a small house and some land in the country. By selling it, they managed to buy a larger, more comfortable house. That's where I was born and spent those first few years.

My parents opened a fabric business and a small haberdashery in our new home. Right there, on the ground floor, my mother fixed and altered clothing and darned stockings to bring in some extra money and add to their savings.

In the village, there was only one doctor for all the houses in the valley, so Mama and Tata helped their sick neighbours for many years. We always had a first aid kit at home containing bandages, aspirin, iodine and ointments.

If I had to define my childhood in Poland, I'd say that it was happy, with our dog Luna and my two dear friends, Analia and Saulo, who were always around for games or to sprint through the shining wheat fields.

I particularly remember the first time we went out to spot the *shabat* star.

It was a pleasantly warm Friday evening, so I encouraged my friends to come out.

"You know what? Yesterday, I came across a book on astronomy."
"Astro-what?" interrupted Saulo.
"Ast-ron-o-my," I spelt out.

"Saulo, it's the study of celestial bodies," clarified Analia. "Our teacher told us the other day, don't you remember?"

"By any chance," I intervened, "do either of you have a torch? Mine has run out of batteries. Although I do have a compass and a map to spot the constellations," I announced.

"Wow!" exclaimed Saulo. "That's all very well, but... counting the stars can make you go blind."

"Baaahhhhh..." answered Analia. "What a load of rubbish! You surely don't believe that?"

"I've got something to show you," I announced in a mysterious voice. "See this book? It belonged to my grandpa David. According to him, a long, long time ago, there were people who used to search the skies for the first star of the *shabat*. The holy day began when they pointed their index finger at the twinkling light and the celebration ended the same way on Saturday evenings."

Saulo piped up, "Hang on a minute... This feels wrong, don't you know that if you point at the sky, then warts will grow on your hands."

"Nonsense!" protested Analia, shaking her head from side to side.

Then all three of us fell about laughing and Luna began to bark excitedly.

We spent a magical evening together scouring the sky. When the weather was good, the four of us used to go in search of our new friends: Cassiopeia, the Great Bear and the Little Bear. As we wound our way home, we danced to the beat of the steadfast lights that shone from the sky, lighting our way home.

I'll keep your secret

Moshé
Poland, 1931

I nearly choked on my birthday cake when I heard Tata and Mama say,

"Moshé, we're moving to Berlin."

They broke it to me just like that, all of a sudden, like a bucket of cold water. When they saw my face, Mama asked,

"Aren't you happy, son?"
"Mama, I think we're happy here. Why leave? Are we moving to a city? We won't know anyone there."
"We'll find it hard to adapt at first but we're doing it for your own good, to give you a better future. The decision's been made," said my father emphatically.

I shot out of the dining room before they could say another word. I just couldn't believe it! They hadn't even asked me! Leaving the village meant that I would never see my friends again and I couldn't imagine that. What's more, what did the big city have to offer us if we were happy here?

I locked myself in my room. My mind was racing, and my heart felt like it was going to burst. It was hard to sleep that night.

The next day, I acted as though nothing was the matter, but I had been hatching a plan - I'd run away with Luna until the whole idea had blown over.

May had already begun, the streets had a different fragrance, and the cold winter was beginning to yield, a good sign that summer was on its way and this would make it easier to run away.

I stealthily gathered a change of clothes plus some food and water. I pocketed the zlotys I'd received for my birthday, and I went to tell my friends the plan.

"Do you want to come with us, Saulo?"
"Are you out of your mind, Moshé? I'd be terrified out there wandering on our own and my parents would ground me for at least a week."
"OK. But don't tell anyone."
"Agreed. I'll keep your secret," said Saulo, slapping the palm of his hand against mine.

From there, I made my way to Analia's house, but she wasn't thrilled by the idea either. I also made her promise not to tell anyone and I set off without either of my friends. Eventually, I felt safe with only Luna trotting alongside me as my bodyguard.

I left the village along the banks of the river that gushed down the Hamin hillside. I crossed the medieval bridge and, once on the other bank, I forked to the right along a narrow path that we used to take in autumn to collect wild mushrooms.

After strolling along for a while, I said to Luna,

"What? Hungry?"

"Woof!" she barked in reply, taking the lead so I could follow her.

"Well, you sound keen. See that patch of woodland ahead? Let's try and make it there to have our lunch and take a break."

Luna wagged her tail enthusiastically and we pressed on.

Right on the edge of the woods, we stopped next to a clear spring. Cupping both my hands, I gave her some water that she quickly lapped up. I stroked her softly just how she liked it, like I did, when Mama stroked my back gently as I pretended to be asleep.

I spotted a polished stone and sat down to open the leftover rice I'd brought from home and share it with my dog. For dessert, we had wild blackberries which tasted sweet and syrupy.

By the position of the sun, I worked out that it would soon be 5 o'clock. We had to get moving if we were going to find somewhere to spend the night. The sky slowly darkened. So, I waved Luna on and readied myself to enter the woods.

All of a sudden, I felt a slight breeze. The leaves seemed to dance on the trees and the birdsong gave us a spectacular concert. Step by step, we picked our way between wild mushrooms of all shapes and sizes. The tall ferns and trees stood like giants at our side, or sentinels guarding the magic of this place.

We had been walking for a long while and, before I knew it, we were lost.

I whipped out my compass and thought it might help us find our way out. I looked for the north, but the needle seemed to have gone mad, spinning round and round. I felt my legs go weak.

"How are we ever going to get home?" I asked out loud looking at Luna.

Little by little, darkness closed in.

Elwinga's watch

Moshé
Poland, 1931

I never thought I'd get lost so easily!

After wandering aimlessly for a while, I realised that there was something familiar about this path - we seemed to be going round in circles. I was cold and my belly had been rumbling for a while.

High above us, the wind was blowing the tops of the lime trees and far away, the menacing howl of wildlife reminded me we weren't alone.

An owl was following us with its beady gaze as it poised loftily on an old branch.

It was then that I remembered the story that Mama used to tell me about fairies and spirits. For a minute, I imagined that we were the characters in the story but, silly me, I'd forgotten to leave a trail of crumbs along the path, so I couldn't find my way back.

So, I got the compass out again and shone my torch on it. It still wasn't working properly. The best thing would be to spend the night there and hope we'd find a way out of this maze in the morning.

I threw a blanket down on the carpet of dead leaves and fell sound asleep. I'd lost all notion of time when Luna woke me up barking insistently. Through the fog of sleep, I shone my torch ahead of me and made out a hazy figure. Luna stood stock-still, growling and barking frantically. My heart was racing and for the first time I knew what fear felt like in my bones.

The silhouette gradually came closer, walking oddly without seeming to touch the floor. Gradually, an old woman appeared before us.

The vigilant owl swooped down from its high branch and perched on her shoulder. Good heavens! That was a surprise!

The old lady spoke clearly to me, asking

"What are you doing here at this time of night, young man? There are prowling wolves at large, dangerously hungry."

"Madame, Luna and I were out for a walk, and we got lost," I stuttered as I trembled. "Please could you show me the way out?"

"I know these woods like the back of my hand young chap, although they get a bit hairy around midnight and it's not a good idea to let the wildlife get wind of you. By the way, you can call me Elwinga. You're welcome to come to my cabin for a cup of the broth I left on the stove before I went out and you can tell me all about yourself."

Something in her look and her voice told me I could trust her, so I decided to accept her invitation.

"Thank you. Both Luna and I could certainly do with warming up."

We scampered behind the mysterious lady who did really seem to know every inch of the woods.

When we arrived, Elwinga nodded to us to enter, flashing us a toothless smile.

"Ummm... so cosy! It smells so good!" I said out loud.

The cabin gave off a pleasant fragrance of spices and my gastric juices told me that, if it wasn't for Elwinga, I'd have gone hungry tonight.

While the old lady stirred the aromatic broth with a huge wooden spoon, she asked me,

"So, what's your name, boy?"
"Moshé, madame. Son of Josek and Clara Abramsky."
"Where are you from?"
"The village nearby. The one with the blue synagogue."
"Ummmm, wait a minute. Your surname rings a bell. I don't know many other Abramskys around here. You wouldn't be the grandson of David and Adira Abramsky, would you?"
"Yes! They were my paternal grandparents, although they died before I was born. Did you know them?"

"Well, well. What a surprise! You don't need to say another word. We used to be neighbours. I was extremely fond of them."

"Please tell me more!"

"You see, in the village where I used to live alongside your grandparents, people always thought I was "strange" because I could see the future. Locals came to my house to be healed and to ask me to read their future. In time, I was accused of witchcraft and people gave me a hard time."

"Witchy-what?"

"You're still too young to understand but, centuries ago, many women were accused of being witches and burnt at the stake."

"Burnt? At the stake?" I couldn't quite believe my ears.

"Yes, although thankfully I didn't actually experience it in the flesh. In a world run by men, wise women were not exactly popular. So, I hold David and Adira in high regard because they cared for me and stood by me through that difficult time. Later, when things got ugly, I took refuge out here."

A supernatural light bathed her face as she spoke, which was strange because it was pitch dark, except for the embers on the fire. Deep down, I considered how difficult it would be to live alone in such a remote spot.

"Well, that's enough chitchat. If I keep on talking like this, I'll end up in tears. Let's have a cup of this wonderful broth! It's bound to warm you up boy," she said with a throaty cackle.

Elwinga produced a loaf of bread from the dresser, served up two steaming cups of broth and we settled by the fire. She had left a serving of soup, soaked in lumps of bread, in a bowl for Luna, who swiftly gobbled it all up.

"You'll see, this broth of boiled bones has been known since time immemorial as 'Jewish penicillin' because it heals and alleviates many ills. For the best results, according to my granny's recipe, it has to simmer for twelve hours."

I don't know exactly how long I spent in that cabin talking with the old lady but before I knew it, the day was breaking. The sun crept in timidly through the tiny window and the cockerels crowed to announce the new day.

"Don't you think it's probably time to be getting home? Your parents must be looking for you and they'll be very worried by now. Come on, I'll come with you to make sure you find the right path."

Luna and I followed Elwinga, running as fast as we could over the grass, amazed as she glided agilely over all the stones.

After a while, she came to a halt and announced.

"We're here. Now you can carry on your own with your doggy without getting lost. This is where we have to say goodbye."

A silvery tear ran down her cheek and she held out her hand to me. She looked me deep in the eye.

"Before you go, I'd like to give you a message to remember always. You'll see, young man, life is continually putting us to the test."

Suddenly, Elwinga closed her eyes, the whisperings of the woods hushed, and a deep silence took hold.

"Never pit yourself against a great force. Wait, take a deep breath and be patient. Sooner or later, it will weaken. When that happens, move forward... take bold strides."

I wondered what Elwinga meant exactly.

Then she rummaged in her bag for an object wrapped in purple velvet and said,

"Look boy, you see this pocket watch? I've had it for a long time. It is unbelievably valuable. It belonged to your grandpa David. He gave it to me in case I ever needed the money. It won't work again until you leave the woods, because there is no concept of time here. From now on, it's yours to keep. Although they are no longer with us, David and Adira would be so happy to know that it's been passed down to you."

Having said that, Elwinga folded me into her arms.

"Farewell, dear Moshé."
"Thank you Elwinga, and farewell."

It was only years later that I understood the real meaning and the importance of that wise woman's message...when Adolf Hitler had already crawled out from under his stone, to the detriment of all humanity.

Back from the woods

Moshé
Poland, 1931

Have you seen Moshé Abramsky? 7 years old. Slim build, wavy brown hair. Last seen with his dog on the morning of 10 May 1931. If you have any information on his whereabouts, please contact the "Abramsky Fabrics" store.

That was the first thing I saw when I reached the village. Our disappearance was on a poster.

"I can't believe it! That's us, Luna! They're looking for us!"

Strangely, the streets were deserted, and my parents weren't home.

There was just one place left to look and that was the synagogue. So, I took the narrow street that wound up the steep hill to our house of prayer.

As I reached the outer esplanade, I heard the babble of voices from inside the temple. I opened the main door and saw Joshua, the rabbi, praying with his arms outstretched, turned to the sky, while everyone else stood to pray. The men and women usually worshiped separately but that day, everyone was in the same room, so I knew that something was afoot.

When the rabbi saw me, his jaw slackened, and his eyes popped out on stalks. He pointed at me, and everyone turned their heads to stare. They all fell silent as I walked in.

Analia and Saulo ran to hug me.

"Moshé, dear friend, we thought you'd gone forever!" exclaimed Saulo.
"Thank goodness you're OK! I was so frightened!" sighed Analia.

Suddenly, other voices piped up,

"It's his ghost! That's not Moshé! A divine appearance!"

Thud! We heard a bump. My mother had fainted.

As I ran to her side, I shouted in annoyance,

"I've only been away a day! What's the fuss!"
"What do you mean, a day, Moshé?" answered Tata irritably. "It's been a whole week!"
"It's a miracle! A miracle!" shouted Rabbi Joshua from the Arc of the Torah.

My mother came round, it was all just a scare. The rabbi drew nearer and ceremoniously took my hand to lead me to the platform of the Sacred Arc.

"Moshé, don't you think you owe your parents an explanation? They have been worried sick for days."

Total silence fell as everyone waited for me to speak.

"My parents decided that we'd go and live in Berlin without asking me," I said, trying to express my point of view.

A low whispering rumbled through the room, getting steadily louder. They probably hadn't yet told their neighbours what they were planning.

"Silence, let Moshé go on," warned the Rabbi.

"Yesterday, I ran away from home because I was really angry. Luna and I walked for a long time and entered a forest. I met a wise woman called Elwinga there who fed us some delicious broth and we talked through the night."

"Let's get to the bottom of this!" exclaimed Joshua. "Now I'm beginning to understand. I've heard that one day inside that forest is the same as a week. It's as though time were just an illusion. As for that woman, she's just a local legend, Moshé. Nothing more."

"That's not true!" I answered in anger. "Elwinga does exist. I can prove it. She told me that for years she was chastised just for being able to see the future. Nevertheless, my grandparents were good to her and helped her out."

"Watch your tongue Moshé," my father stepped in, raising his voice, "My parents never talked to me about that woman. If it were true, I'd have known about it."

"Tata! I wouldn't lie to you!" I protested. "Luna and I got lost. Shortly after, the old lady turned up... If it weren't for her, we'd still be lost or who knows what.

You only have to listen to the howling wolves... It'd give you goosebumps."

"God in Israel! The child has gone mad!" cried one of the neighbours.

Straight away, I put my hand in my pocket and brought out the wise woman's gift.

"Here's the proof that I've not gone mad. This watch belonged to my grandfather and Elwinga gave it to me," I said, showing it to him. "You can see the name of David Abramsky engraved on it and his date of birth, 1868."

Tata took the cold, round item in his hands and began to sob, grasping it to his chest.

High in the rafter of the synagogue, an owl kept its beady eyes on me, and I felt as though Elwinga's soul was watching over us.

The Abramsky family arrives in Berlin

Moshé
Berlin, 1931

It's easy to fall in love at first sight with a city like Berlin, even more so for a boy like me, fresh from the countryside. Everything moves so fast. The trams are fit to burst, and the city is packed with shops, cafés and restaurants.

That was my first impression although I swiftly encountered the bitter side of Berlin. Germany had been trying to get itself back on its feet for years following World War One and the Great Depression of 1929 that had left many people struggling in poverty.

The day that we arrived, our village rabbi sent his friend Ashir to meet us at the station.

We loaded our suitcases onto his van. Luna was barking frantically, alert to ever possible danger.

"Moshé, can you calm that dog down please! If she goes on like that, everyone will stare at us," ordered my father. "I don't know if it was such a great idea to bring her."
"Calm down darling. Without Luna, Moshé wouldn't have wanted to come, and he'd be in a terrible mood," ensured Mama, in an attempt to keep the peace.

My mother knew that I saw our dog as one of the family and I couldn't have left her at home for anything in the world.

Ashir started up the vehicle that coughed coal-black smoke as it drove off. As we motored along, the rabbi's pal gave us a quick tour through the streets, enthusiastically pointing out the most important monuments in our new city.

"Look! That's the Brandenburg Gate," he said, nodding ahead. "It's a true symbol of this tireless city. You haven't really visited the city without seeing it."

Unfortunately, we arrived in Berlin at a time when immigrants were not exactly the flavour of the month. Some industries had closed down making many people unemployed. The idea was gradually blooming in Germany that we were coming to steal their jobs, but nothing was further from the truth because Tata and Mama intended to open their own business there.

Our early days were tough. People were unkind and indifferent to us when they heard our strong Polish accents trying to speak German. What's more, many landlords gave us the run-around or set really high prices to put us off but my parents were very determined.

In the meantime, we lived in Berlin with Ashir and his family, very close to Oranienburger Strasse. He and his wife Ruth were German Jews and, thanks to their kindness, we quickly met the Jewish community at the Rykestrasse synagogue.

"Get ready to see a temple so big, it won't look like any you've ever seen in Poland. Tomorrow, you'll see it with your own eyes," said Ashir with a chuckle.

The next day was Friday and my parents arranged to go to Rykestrasse to pray and meet the Rabbi.

Walking in there for the first time really took my breath away. Ashir wasn't exaggerating, far from it! As soon as I stepped inside, my attention was caught by the high nave that created a central passageway with two rows of benches, left and right. Our village synagogue was tiny compared to this vast temple.

Rykestrasse was the meeting point for Jews in Berlin. We mainly went there to celebrate the *kabalat shabat*, the start of *shabat*, on Fridays. I made friends whenever I went, because Tata and Mama were understanding and let me play for a while with the other kids during the religious ceremony. Sometimes, I also took part in a short reading of the Torah.

As for our daily lives at Ashir's house, there were a few changes that I wasn't so keen on. As Orthodox Jews, they observed their religion strictly, unlike my parents, who believed that Judaism should adapt to modern times and be more flexible.

Therefore, while we were living there, we had to fit in with their strict daily practices. To give just one example, in the kitchen they used different sets of plates - one for meat and the other for dairy products. What's more, they only ate meat if it was pure, purchased at *kosher* butchers, which meant that it was suitable according to Jewish law.

By the time we'd been there a month, I was looking forward to a little privacy and my own room, like our old house back in the village. One afternoon, as the three of us were walking Luna, Mama said,

"We've got a surprise for you. Tomorrow, we're going to see a house owned by the parents of a good friend of Ashir, who told us that it's really great. If we like it, we'll rent it and then go out and buy bread and salt."

"Bread and salt…" I queried.

"Yes son, it's an ancient Jewish custom. Bread is a basic element and stands for riches. Salt symbolises purity," mama told me, placing her right hand on her heart.

"You mean that it will bring us good luck?"

"That's it," she answered, nodding her head.

"And another thing son, your mother and I would love to listen to you play your violin at our house-warming. Why don't you play us a Polish tune for a special day? It would be like bringing a tiny bit of our country here."

"Yes, Tata. I'll play the mazurca that Mama taught me! I replied, pleased.

"That´ll make me so happy! You're a good boy, Moshé. But, ah! Of course, we'll have to go through with our family's cockerel tradition!"

"Did you say cockerel?"

"Yes son, before we move in, the new house should have been lived in by a cockerel."

"Whaaat?" I asked in amazement.

"You heard. So, when we know if we can have the house, you can come with me to the market to pick the cockerel you like best," announced my father, slapping me on the back.

Three days later, Tata, Luna and I headed out first thing to buy the animal, without ever imagining the adventure we would have that day.

"What a cockerel! It won't hold still! Moshé, grab the cage we brought so it doesn't get away!"

Suddenly Luna let out a loud bark. The bird had escaped the shopkeeper's clutches with a sharp peck on the arm and flown out of the front door. Luna barked tirelessly as she followed it down the street.

What a start to our move! My dog was chasing a splendid cockerel with shiny feathers through the streets of Berlin while Tata and I ran behind.

House-warming

Moshé
Berlin, 1931

It seemed as though the day would never come, but finally we could move into our new house. We were really looking forward to holding the *janukat habait*, our house-warming ritual. We chose a Tuesday because tradition dictates that this would bring us luck and prosperity.

As soon as our guests arrived, the rabbi began to pray and bless our house. He fitted a little scroll called a *mezuzá* in a small box. This is an amulet that protects the home and the people that live there.

"Moshé, my son, the *mezuzá* on the door frame shows that this is a Jewish home and also reminds us of the importance of our faith."

"Will the *mezuzá* stay on the door forever?"

"Yes, it should be firmly fastened to the frame," ensured my father. "Watch how they do it so the two of us can fit them on all the doors in the house later," smiled Tata. Meanwhile, the rabbi was fastening the little box with a hammer and nails to the right of the main doorway.

Then, one by one, our close friends wished us wealth and happiness in our life in this new home.

Once the ceremony was over, my friends and I read a short passage from the Torah under the watchful eye of the adults. Then we sat down at the table to eat but before we began, Tata and Mama thanked everyone for coming.

Ashir surprised us by preparing a tasty *kosher* lamb with couscous and raisins. It's one of my favourite dishes. For dessert, we ate *strudel* made with quince jelly and almonds by my mother, which was deliciously sweet. As they brought it out, my parents announced that their son, that's me, would play mazurcas, waltzes and polonaises on the violin that soon got everyone up and dancing.

It turned out to be an extraordinary day and a great way to start life in our new home in Berlin.

Adolf Hitler:

Dictator and ruler of Nazi Germany. Directly responsible for the death of millions of people, mainly Jews. Master orator, he was supported by Germans at a time of economic, political and social crisis.

My life in Berlin

Moshé
Berlin, 1933

We'd been in Berlin for a full two years, but I still couldn't get used to the change.

My school was boring, and my classmates turned their noses up at foreigners. They particularly despised Jews. Otto, my tutor, was nothing like Andrzej, my teacher in Poland. Here, it was all about rules and punctuality in an exaggerated, overwhelming way.

One Friday at the synagogue, I heard Ashir whispering with my father.

"The Jewish community is very worried, Josek."
"What are you talking about Ashir?"
"Adolf Hitler and his Nazi party are gaining popularity, tuning into the nation's grumbles. They are promising people a better Germany, although all these ideas on racial superiority are the most worrying."
"Exactly, Ashir, I feel like this country is changing," my father answered in a concerned tone.
"I fear that this man has more people with him than against him and that people will flock to vote him in at the next elections. I don't know if he's aware it's common knowledge that he hates the Jews. Look, Josek, if what people tell me about Hitler is true, we'll have to watch our backs in the not-too-distant future."

His words foretold what was soon to happen, as all these fears came true. On 30 January 1933, the sky turned leaden like I'd never seen before in Berlin. That was the day Hitler came to power and brought all our misfortune with him.

That afternoon, as I was listening to the new Chancellor giving his inaugural speech on the radio, fatefully declaring that "Jews are undoubtedly a race, but they are not human," I saw fear flash across my parents' faces. I knew it because they gripped each other's hand tightly and did not let go for a long time.

I realised something was wrong immediately and asked,

"Mama, if this gentleman is so evil, why did so many people vote for him?"

"Son, Hitler is a powerful speaker and knows how to captivate the population, who are desperately pleading for change. His manifesto and his speeches have promised people a better life and a new, glorious Germany."

"Why does he talk about our Jewish community so much?"

"He wants to convince the Germans that we are the root of all their problems," said my mother.

"Ummmm. I don't get it," I answered.

"You'll see, Hitler wants to close Jewish businesses, but people will realise that he's wrong and won't pay any attention," explained Tata.

"So, nobody will come and buy fabric from our store?"

"Don't worry, his bark is worse than his bite. I have a feeling that this chap won't last long in power," answered my father, trying to calm us down.

Change was slow and gradual. It threatened our very survival, and we didn't see it coming in time. We clung to the mistaken idea that it would all blow over soon but the devil in person was amongst us.

Things started to happen...

One morning, we found our shop window had been daubed with the star of David and a poster that read in large letters: Don't shop in Jewish stores.

The Nazis came to town like a herd of elephants. From one day to the next, they made us do the German salute with our arm out at school, shouting "Heil Hitler!" between fifty and hundred times a day. If you didn't do it properly, you were flogged or suspended from school for a week.

There were many changes... For example, now we went out to the playground more often for physical education. Otto often stopped class to take us to the assembly hall to watch a film on the Third Reich.

I'd begun to have my fill of der Führer!

As the days went by, I realised that Alexander and Emilia were missing. They were schoolteachers who sat next to us at the Rykestrasse synagogue. We were told that they had been expelled from education for promoting "undesirable" ideas among young people.

I wondered how they would live now.

Shortly afterwards, as soon as school began, the headmaster gathered us together to give us some news.

"I'd like to introduce you to two young teachers who will be joining our school. They have been selected by the Government and I can't think of a better way of welcoming them than singing the Nazi party anthem in their honour." So, with due solemnity, we stood in the pouring rain and sang for a long while, repeating the song over and over, soaked to the skin. That day, I was wet through when I got home.

The next morning, I asked Otto where Alexander and Emilia were. Without the slightest explanation, he punished me by making me stand with my arms outstretched before the portrait of der Führer until my arms gave way. When I got home, I didn't want to tell my parents about it because it would only worry them.

Some students' obsessions to please Adolf Hitler reached unthinkable extremes. Once, as we lined up to go inside, Martina from year 4 fainted in her row. I later found out that she belonged to the Bundesverband Deutscher Milchviehhalter (the German Girls League) and had been suffering from a stomach-ache for two days. In the end, she died from appendicitis. She hadn't complained because der Führer didn't like moaners.

It became a daily ritual for Otto to laugh at us for being Jews in front of our classmates. One day he asked excruciatingly shy Alfred if he knew the meaning of the word "bastard" as we were studying "pure blood" in Natural Sciences. Some of us were stunned as we heard our teacher say that this student was a living example of a "bastard" because he had a Jewish father and a German mother. Otto used to constantly play the same music on the gramophone in his classes. It was an opera by Wagner who believed that music was the best antidote to human impurities.

Wanting to pile more shame on those of us with Jewish blood, that day he made us each recite part of the text on human reproduction twenty times that said, "*Each species must be attracted by the same species and procreate with the same species.*"

Germans were considered to be a superior race and branded us inferior.

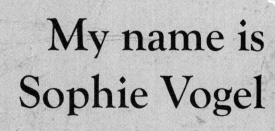

My name is
Sophie Vogel

Wannsee - Germany

My name is Sophie Vogel. I was born in 1926 in Wannsee, to the southeast of Berlin, Germany. My father is called Frank, my mother Anne, and my maternal grandmother, Irene. Like mine, her name comes from Greek and means 'peace'. You can't help but love my Omi as soon as you meet her because she's one of those people with a gift to smooth out life's problems. What's more, we have a special link between us, like an invisible thread joining us.

Mutti told me that Omi was the first person to hold me when I was born. Back then, my father began to travel more due to his job in the family business, so Omi came over to our house more often to help out. We loved having her over and I was always cuddling up to her and gurgling in delight.

The only problem was that she and my father used to clash because they thought so differently, which bothered Mutti. When he came back from one of his trips, something happened that proved to be the final straw. This time Omi Irene packed her bag in silence. Mutti and I had tears in our eyes as we watched her go, but she tried to lighten the tone by reminding us of our invisible thread.

I hope that I grow up to be like her and always laugh out loud, inviting my good friends over for tea and chatting freely about our lives.

As for Opi Wolfgang, my maternal grandfather, I only know that he left one day when Omi was pregnant and Mutti never knew him. One time, I asked Omi Irene about him, and the silent furrowing of her brow told me that she'd rather not talk about him.

As for my paternal grandparents, Bettina and Thorsten, they died of a strange flu that killed many people throughout Europe. Vati was adopted by a rich family with very traditional ideals who passed down their order, discipline and authoritarian character to him. I feel sorry for him when I think about his sad, difficult childhood.

Concentration camps:

detention centres where people are held, against the law. They were built in Nazi Germany from 1933 onwards.

What they didn't want to tell me

Sophie
Berlin, 1933

I met Moshé when I was seven years old. It was around the time that we moved from Wannsee to Friedrichstrasse, in the Mitte district.

Moving to a new home was no cause for celebration for me, although according to my parents "we'd live right in the centre, and we'd have excellent views of the city." Vati had recently landed a job as a civil engineer for the Government, which he combined with the family business. Living in Friedrichstrasse meant he could walk to his office.

When we got to our new building, there was nobody to welcome us. It seemed like everyone minded their own business in Berlin. Even when I met a neighbour on the stairs, they greeted me curtly and went on their way. In Wannsee, everybody knew everybody.

Time went by and I still missed living by the lakes. And I missed my Omi of course, as she had lived close by. One day I worked up the courage to tell Vati how I felt,

"I miss our old life. Berlin is so big that I find it hard to make new friends."

"My girl, this city will bring us many opportunities, believe me. I'm sure you'll meet other German boys and girls soon in your new school. Please be patient. Sophie, good things come to those who wait."

"I understand, father," I nodded, although not entirely convinced, hoping he was right.

As time went on, my father began to travel more frequently to the south of Germany, to the city of Dachau. He used to stay there for a week at a time, sometimes longer.

During one of his trips, my curiosity got the better of me and I asked Mutti,

"Why does Vati go there so often?"

"According to what he tells me, he's running a big engineering project that will be really good for our country; it's State business so the fewer people who know about it, the better, Sophie."

For a while, I wondered what was so important that they didn't want to tell me.

The day I met Moshé

Sophie
Berlin, 1933

After living in Berlin for a while, something unexpected happened...

As I recall, it was a Thursday and Mutti had picked me up from school, like always. She needed some fabric for new curtains, and she remembered a store on the way home where she could get material at a decent price.

"If I'm not mistaken, this is it," she said, pointing to a shop called "Abramsky Fabrics".

The streets were chaotic at this time of day. We stopped in front of the small shop window displaying colourful fabrics; I rang the bell, and we immediately heard the sound of footsteps.

"Please come in, girls," a boy with dark curly hair welcomed us, with his hand held to his chest.

From a small counter, an adult nodded their welcome and then addressed the child in a serious tone,

"Son, haven't we taught you to respect your elders? You shouldn't speak to this lady as if she were a youngster."
"You're right, father. Please excuse my bad manners, Madame," he uttered with a deep blush.

My mother immediately quipped back, "Please, don't scold the boy for that. He actually made me feel young again," she answered, winking at the boy, who reddened again.

"Please excuse me. I don't think that my son should take liberties. We haven't brought him up to be cheeky at home."

Later, while Mutti looked at the fabrics that the shopkeeper patiently brought out for her, the curly-haired boy and I struck up conversation.

"Where do you live?" he asked inquisitively. "I haven't seen you around here."

"I live a few blocks away, in Friedrichstrasse. We just moved in and we're still exploring this area. Actually, we barely know the city. Have you ever been to Wannsee, in the southeast? That's where we used to live."

"Ahh! I've never been, although some of Tata's friends have talked about the lakes there. But tell me, do you really live in that street?" he asked me with a look of amazement.

"Of course. Why wouldn't I?"

"Because we live right there as well and you and I have never met before today," the boy answered enthusiastically.

"I live at number five, Friedrichstrasse."

"Wow!" What a coincidence! We're practically neighbours. We live at number four," he smiled in surprise.

"What about you? Where do you go once you've done your homework?"

"I don't go out much, except with my parents and when my Omi comes to stay. It's hard to make friends in such a big city where everyone seems in such a hurry. At least I have Hannah, a teacher that I met at my new school. Just like me, she's an only child and although she's older, we always have stuff to chat about. I talk to her like she's my big sister."

"I'm glad that you've already got someone in Berlin to spend time with. Now, if you want, you've got another friend in me," said the boy pointing to his chest. "What's more, you and I have plenty in common. I don't have any brothers or sisters either, so you can come over and play at my house whenever you want. Maybe you could help me with my German. You might have noticed that I still find it hard to pronounce some words."

"Oh, yes, thank you! I'd love to! I've been feeling a bit lonely since we got to Mitte. Everything was easier in Wannsee where I also used to spend more time with my grandmother. And of course, I can help you out with your pronunciation to improve your German."

"The same thing happened to me, and I found it hard to fit in when we arrived in Germany. In Poland, where I was born, I left behind two close friends, Saulo and Analia. But little by little, I've been making new friends here.

"By the way, you haven't told me your name," said the boy, seriously.

"Sophie Vogel", I answered and immediately felt my cheeks burning.

"That's a very pretty name," said the boy, stroking his chin. Suddenly, his father butted into our conversation, "Miss, did you know that your name comes from Greek and means 'wisdom'?"

"Yes, sir. That's what my Omi tells me, she's called Irene."

The shopkeeper gave the hint of a smile and continued showing my mother other fabrics.

"What about you? What's your name?" I asked the boy.

"Moshé Abramsky."

"Ummmm. That has a ring to it. I like it."

"Thank you, Sophie. My name is a variant of Moses and comes from Hebrew."

"Ah! I had no idea," I answered.

"You talk about your grandmother a lot - you must miss her."

"I do. What's more, she and I are joined by an invisible thread," I confessed with a tiny smile.

"An invisible thread? I don't understand how you can be joined to someone by something you can't see," exclaimed the boy, scratching his chin again.

"You'll see, when you love someone in a special way, although you can't see or touch that affection, you can feel it deep inside you. That's why it's invisible," I explained to Moshé. He gave me a broad smile and his eyes shone like bright morning stars.

Meanwhile, my mother was having a lively chat with Josek - that was the name of my new friend's father. He was telling Mutti that they were from a village and had come to Berlin in search of a better life, so their son could study. Leaving their beloved Poland behind was no easy task for the Abramsky family and they had sacrificed a lot to open their small fabric business.

Since we'd come to the big city, this was the first time that two people had stopped to talk to us so cheerily.

When they lit the gas lamps in the street, Mutti reminded me that we had to be going. It was almost dinner time.

Before leaving the store, Moshé's dad turned his bright gaze on us and said,

"*Shalom*. Please return whenever you wish."

"Thank you. You have both been so friendly, we have had a lovely time," my mother replied gratefully.

"What does *shalom* mean?" I asked as soon as we stepped on to the pavement.

"It's their greeting."

"A Polish greeting?"

"No darling, that's how Jews greet each other," my mother explained and continued, "the Abramsky are emigrants. Did you know Sophie that there are half a million Jews in Berlin alone?"

"Wow!" And do they all come to our country 'to make their dreams come true'?"

"Moshé's parents, like so many other people, left their country more out of need than choice. Do you understand what that means?"

"Yes Mutti! I think they must have been very brave to make a decision like that. Tomorrow, I'm going to tell Hannah that I've made a new friend from a Jewish family. I told you, didn't I?"

"What have you told me, dear?"

"That her maternal grandparents were Jewish, and she was born in France."

"I didn't know that, Sophie."

Mutti put her arm around my shoulders, and we walked home. I had started to like Berlin a tiny bit more now that I had met Moshé.

The day I met Sophie

Moshé
Berlin, 1933

Sophie burst into my life like a lovely surprise one afternoon when she appeared in our shop with her mother.

People from our neighbourhood came to our shop which sold all sorts of fabrics exclusively imported from abroad. I almost always went over after lunch to help out. I liked to sit by Tata and welcome the customers. It made me feel grown up! I suppose I would be about 9 years old then, but people always thought I was older because of my height.

Shortly after Sophie and her mother went home, we realised that they had left a letter on the counter. I shot out to search for them, but I couldn't spot them in the crowded street.

"Moshé, you must take this letter to the Vogel house. They are probably looking for it and at least we know where they live," said my father as he handed over the envelope.

In truth, the chore brightened my afternoon because it meant I would see Sophie again. As I walked over, I read that the letter was intended for a government bigwig and I supposed that the sender, a man's name with the surname of Vogel, would be the father of the girl with flaxen hair.

When I arrived at my destination, the building door was opened by a skinny, hunched man, with a bad-tempered face.

"What brings you here, boy?" he asked sharply.

"I have come to return this letter to the Vogel family," I showed him the envelope and saw his frown relax.

"Go ahead, young man. Up you go, it's on the fourth floor, on the left. The lady and her daughter are at home," he assured me in a friendly tone.

I climbed the steep stairs up to the fourth floor and rang the bell.

"Who is it?" asked Sophie on the other side of the door.

"It's Moshé, the boy from the fabric store. I'm bringing you something you left on the counter."

Sophie opened the door straight away and invited me into the sitting room.

"Mutti, it's the boy from the Abramsky store. He's brought Vati's letter."

"Oh, young man!! What good news! I couldn't think where I might have left it! It was an urgent errand from my husband, and it should be at the Post Office already," said Sophie's mother, letting out a sigh of relief. "I'm really grateful. How can I thank you? Darling, how about we get some biscuits for...? Excuse me, what was your name again?"

"Moshé, at your service."

While Sophie helped her mother get the tea ready, I was left alone for a few moments. I scrutinised the huge, spotless living room. A glass door stood slightly ajar. I drew near and peeped through the crack. It was a narrow office, with a desk covered in plans and maps, different sizes of rulers, set squares and compasses. Next to it, on a small side table, there stood a bottle of liqueur and an ashtray full of cigarette ends. A portrait hung on the central wall of a serious looking man, with a trim jet-black moustache and penetrating eyes that seemed to follow me around the room. It was none other than Adolf Hitler!! I couldn't believe my eyes.

I jumped as I heard the front door open, and I quickly sat down in the living room. A gentleman of medium build, dressed in a black suit and tie, was examining me strangely.

"Hello, who are you?" he asked, looking me up and down.

Suddenly, I heard Frau Vogel's voice as she came in from the kitchen carrying a plate piled with biscuits and two glasses of milk. She was followed by Sophie.

"Hello dear, this is Moshé, the son of the Abramskys, from the neighbourhood fabric store. He came to return the letter I left there when we were shopping for material this afternoon.

Moshé, this is Frank, my husband."
"Pleased to meet you, sir."

Herr Vogel did not return my greeting and I saw his face stiffen tensely.

"Anne, we need to talk. Please step into the bedroom."

I was so embarrassed when Sophie and I were left alone. I remember it as if it were yesterday, with her innocent smile and her special fragrance of fresh flowers.

Blushing, not knowing quite what to say, I ventured,

"Your house is very nice."
"Thanks. We've not been in Berlin very long, like I told you in the store. Actually, it was my father's decision, now that he's working for the government and his office is just a few minutes away. Would you like some milk and biscuits?" the girl asked me.
"Yum... I'd love some! You know, when I'm on my own at home, I usually dunk them in the milk but if Mama saw me doing that, she'd tell me to mind my manners," I winked.

While Sophie went to the kitchen for sugar, from the living room I could clearly make out the Vogels' voices from the bedroom. I was astonished to hear my own name raised in their conversation.

"What's this about dear?"

"Do you know how much trouble I'd be in if anyone had read this letter? You must be more careful."

"I'm sorry, it won't happen again. But tell me, why is it so important?"

"As you know full well, I have to keep everything to do with my work and position absolutely top secret. Furthermore, as things stand, you'd better not shop in the Abramsky's store anymore. I don't want the neighbours to see us with them. The Führer's men are almost certainly investigating where these businesses have sprung up from. Get rid of this Moshé as soon as you can, don't let our daughter get fond of him."

Anne turned to Sophie who was coming back with a small bowl overflowing with sugar cubes,

"Darling, you need to get on with your homework, it will get dark soon and Moshé needs to go home."

"Please Mutti, leave us a little longer, we've hardly had the chance to chat. I'll study later, I promise."

"Don't make a fuss Sophie," her mother said, dropping her gaze. "Come on Moshé, I'll show you out."

"What's the hurry all of a sudden?" asked the girl, in a bewildered gesture.

I barely had time to say goodbye to my new friend. When we were on the landing, Anne handed me a folded note from her skirt pocket. Bringing her head close to my ear, she whispered a warning,

"Young man, give this note to your father and remind him that he should destroy it once he's read it." Her face was deadly serious.

"Yes, madame, I'll do that." I said goodbye with a "*shalom*," which means 'peace go with you' in my language.

As I heard the keys locking the door behind me, my curiosity got the better of me and I stopped to read the note. It said 'Herr Abramsky, please take care. You are probably being watched by the Government.'

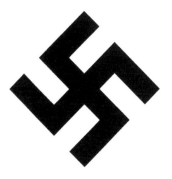

Fascism:

intolerant and racist political movement that opposes democracy. Fascism uses violence to impose its ideas and eliminates or represses anyone who thinks differently.

It will be
our secret

Sophie
Berlin, 1933

"Sophie, please, I don't want you spending time with strange people," Vati warned me as Moshé left the house.

"Vater, he came here to return a letter that Mutti was going to take to the Post Office."

"He could just have left it with the doorman," he said forcefully. "I don't think it's a good idea to let foreigners into our home."

"Of course Adam let him into the building, it's his job, and we should be grateful to Moshé and his father for their kindness. What's more, they were very good to us in their store," I explained to my father, hoping that I would win him over with these extra details.

Vati said nothing. He had a faraway look in his eyes. When he pulled himself together, he warned me sternly,

"Sophie, you don't understand yet because you're still a child. Among other things, Jews have come here to get rich at our expense and they pose a real danger for Germany's well-being."

"But Vati, both you and Mutti are always telling me to love my neighbour. Tell me what's wrong with being friends with the Abramsky family?"

My father was pensive for a while, as he cleaned his glasses meticulously.

"Sophie, I'm very concerned about your education and who you spend time with. Having foreign friends, especially Jews, will do you no favours, believe me," he expounded as if giving a speech. Then he used his intimidating voice to warn me, "You're still too young to separate the sheep from the goats but I hope you forget all about that boy. Concentrate on your schoolwork and act like a young German lady with exquisite manners."

Vati sighed, murmured something under his breath that I couldn't catch and furrowed his brow again.

"Sophie, that boy is not the same as us. As an adult, I have to look out for your well-being, and I know that being friends with a Jew will only cause you problems. Let's not speak of this again, you are forbidden to see him."

"But Vater!" I protested, refusing to be intimidated by his words this time. "Omi always tells me that everyone is equal in the eyes of the world. What we hold in our hearts is the most important."

He did not care for my answer one little bit, all the more so for mentioning Omi Irene with whom he rarely saw eye to eye. His face flushed and he folded his arms angrily, staying that way for what seemed like an eternity. His cutting words made me want to burst into tears but the lump in my throat stopped them from coming. I stared at my feet and clenched my fists, determined that I would not shed one tear in front of him.

By the time I could bring myself to tell him how wrong he was, he had already turned on his heels and was stalking back down the corridor, muttering to himself.

I stood stock still, watching him slip into the room he had set up as an office although it was really a cage that he locked himself into for hours to work at home. If I was sure of one thing, it was that working for the government and his new friendships had changed him.

I fled to the bathroom, closed the door and burst into tears. My mother must have heard me because she came in without knocking.

"Sophie, what on earth is wrong?"
"It's nothing Mutti," I answered in distress.
"What do you mean 'nothing', darling? I hardly ever see you in such a state. Something really serious must have happened. Whatever it is, you can tell me."
"I know," I sobbed.

I sat up and she began to stroke my plaits, with the kind of tenderness that is so hard to put into words. As she dried my tears, I recounted my conversation with Vati.

"I don't understand. Moshé and his father were so kind to us. Just as I've found someone to study and play with, why should I care what Vater thinks of Jews or foreigners?" I whined.

My mother's eyes widened like dinner plates. She was silent for a couple of minutes, lost in thought... her mind seemed to be straying far from the bathroom.

In a low voice, she confessed,

"Sophie, your father is more engrossed in his own world every day. I've noticed that he seems more and more confused and withdrawn and I think that it's partly down to his work and his new colleagues," my mother confirmed my own theory. "How about we give him a little time? He'll come around, I'm sure of it. He probably thought that staying away from Moshé is the best thing for you and sometimes adults can make mistakes, despite our good intentions."

My mother reached into her apron pocket and produced a handkerchief embroidered with her initials to dry my tears.

"Darling, I won't stop you if you want to see your friend. It will be our secret. As for Vati, time will tell." Mutti hugged me and kissed my left ear lobe.
"I'd like that, Mutti. Thanks! It will be our secret."

I pressed my chest against hers. Despite the darkness, when I looked up at her, I saw her eyes twinkling. That twinkle felt like a blessing.

Hannah, the teacher

Sophie
Berlin, 1933

When I arrived in Friedrichstrasse in 1933, my parents enrolled me at a mixed public school they had been recommended, renowned for its strict discipline and national values.

That's where I met Hannah, a woman who really made a big impression on me. Despite our age difference, she became my best friend in Berlin.

My memories of her are her syrupy voice, jet black eyes and the infinite kindness she radiated. She was born in a poor neighbourhood of Paris and had been living in Germany for the last five years. Although she spoke our language perfectly, sometimes without realising it, she let slip the occasional expression in French like "*C'est la vie!*" It made the whole class crack up and she laughed along with us.

Over time, almost without realising it, we had forged a beautiful friendship. This meant we could often talk "girl to girl" and Hannah seemed like the big sister I'd never had.

One day as we were chatting, I brought up something that had been on my mind.

"My father wants to send me to a summer camp, organised by the German Girls' League. He says that these days our country needs disciplined women who are healthy and strong."

"Are you going to go, Sophie?" my teacher asked me, wide-eyed.

"I'm not sure. I don't know the other girls and I've promised Omi that I'd spend the summer with her. Would you go, Hannah?"

"Sophie, it's up to you to decide whether you feel like it or not."

"Have you ever been away to camp?" I asked my teacher curiously.

"Yes, back in France, but not that type of camp. I've heard that these camps teach German girls to feel superior to other races, like the best people in the world, the most efficient, the most beautiful... It's completely unreal."

"Ohhh!" I exclaimed, and shivers ran down my spine.

"Sophie, your father probably thinks that this kind of experience is the best thing for you. My advice would be to listen to the little voice inside you and decide for yourself."

I didn't have to think very hard to answer my friend and teacher.

"Thank you! You've been a great help. I'll tell Vati that I'm not interested."

Hannah's advice stayed with me like a catchy tune playing over and over in my heart for a long time.

Dots and dashes

Moshé
Berlin, 1933

It had only been two days since I'd met Sophie and already, I needed to see her again. I dashed off a note to her that I handed to Adam.

"Hi! It's Moshé. Do you want to come over and play tomorrow?"

Adam, her building's doorman, was a bit cantankerous but I suspect he had a soft spot for me, particularly because, next time, he greeted me with a wink and flashed me a glimpse of his brown false teeth.

At lunchtime, as I made my way home from school, Adam called me over.

"Come here, boy! How was your day? Listen... You're quite the lucky chap!" he said a little sarcastically. "Sophie left this for you." He stretched out his bony hand and gave me a sealed envelope that smelt of flowers.

I thanked the doorman and crossed back over the road to my building. I told Mama about it as soon as I got home, gleefully waving the letter.

"Look, it's from Sophie! The girl I told you about the other day."

"A letter? What's that about Moshé? What happened?"

"Nothing Mama. I wrote to her this morning to see if she wanted to play with me and she wrote back."

"I thought something terrible had happened, but never mind, go on and read it!"

I threw myself down on the sofa and prised it open, trying not to rip the envelope. I pulled out a single sheet of paper and began to read. I couldn't believe my eyes - the text was just dots and dashes! A dot and two dashes; a dot and three dashes and a dot, on and on until the very end. The only thing I could understand was the word MORSE, written in capital letters. "Sophie is having a good laugh at my expense," I mused.

Unsure what to do with her reply, I gave the letter to Tata to read as soon as he walked in the door. He stared hard at the paper and after a while, he broke into a chuckle.

"Moshé, you poor thing. Don't worry," he said, stroking my head to calm me down. "Sophie has written to you in Morse code."

"Morse?" I asked, hanging my head.

"Son, it's an alphabet where each letter has an equivalent in a code using dots and dashes that are transmitted using sounds."

"Code?" I ventured curiously.

"It means that you have to decipher it to understand it. You'll see, the signals vary in length and are represented by dots and dashes. You know what? The telegraph was a great invention and meant that two points far away could communicate with each other. I promise to help you after lunch, but first we'll take a look at the book your grandfather used when he passed his exams to work in the Post Office. There's bound to be a section on Morse code."

My father treasured my grandfather David's belongings, now including the watch that wise Elwinga gave me in the woods.

"Look, Moshé! Here's the chapter on Morse code," said Papa enthusiastically, pointing to a page in the book.

Like a spy game, we sat down to solve the puzzle and it took us all afternoon to finish the text, deciphering the message as 'Hi Moshé! I'd love to play with you. I'll come to your house tomorrow at five o'clock.'

"You lucky boy!" Papa smiled.

Only then could I jump for joy knowing I'd see Sophie the next day. That night I fell into a deep, peaceful sleep, dreaming of dots and dashes.

The Abramsky family

Sophie
Berlin, 1933

I wasn't going to give up on Moshé just because my father didn't want me to be friends with a Jewish boy. I found it hard to understand his way of thinking and his argument seemed ridiculously unfair. It was probably just his new job making him like this, more reserved and authoritarian. So, if I wanted to see Moshé, my only option was to hide the truth from Vater and make him believe that his daughter had come around to his way of thinking.

Moshé and I often used to meet up like this, except for Sundays and the very few afternoons that Vati was at home. We wove our lasting friendship in secret.

In contrast, Josek and Clara welcomed me with open arms, making me feel like one of the family.

"Won't you stay for dinner tonight, Sophie? My wife has made some exquisite fish cakes with a lemon and egg sauce. You'll see, they're really tasty," my friend's father assured me.

"I'd like nothing better, but Vati is due back from his trip. Another time, I hope Josek," I answered sadly.

"Of course," Clara smiled. "You'll be over tomorrow, won't you Sophie? We're so happy that you're Moshé's friend. When we left Poland, we were worried that he'd find it hard to fit in here, far from his childhood friends Saulo and Analia. Thankfully, it's been quite the opposite and now he has you too."

I blushed helplessly at that, feeling like hundreds of butterflies were fluttering in my stomach.

"Thank you, Mrs Abramsky. I'll be back tomorrow. The same thing happened to me when I came here from Wannsee. And I also like being friends with your son."

Although we went to different schools, we used to study together in the afternoon. He helped me out with tricky subjects like Maths; and I gave him a hand with German grammar. After our homework, we always had a little time to play or talk about important stuff we wanted to share with each other.

So, thanks to our trust, acceptance, understanding and affection for each other, our friendship grew stronger day by day and Moshé quickly became a very important person in my life.

Herr Albert and the new directives

Sophie
Berlin, 1933 - 1934

As time went by, things came to happen that would not only affect Germany but also Moshé's life, and mine.

At the start of the new school year, the new headmaster marched into class one morning, sticking out his right hand, earnestly shouting "Sieg Heil". It reminded me of one of my father's colleagues who we had bumped into as we left the house one day.

"Good morning. My name is Herr Albert. I will be in charge of this school from now on," he announced as he scrutinised us with his tiny eyes, like a vicious little hedgehog. "I'm going to apply a series of directives for the new German school model that we will be following now."
"What are directives, sir?" asked the teacher's pet.
"They are a list of rules, young man, instructions given for a purpose. They will furnish you with the education that this country deserves. Germany will soon be the looking glass that the rest of the world wishes to gaze into," he ensured us solemnly.

Then he glanced at his watch and announced

"You'll be happy to know that we will spend more time on Physical Education. The Führer wants the Aryan race to dominate Europe and so we have to get physically stronger. This will help the boys become young athletes and the girls, excellent gymnasts."

As Herr Albert was droning on and on, I began to wonder about what it meant to be a "dominant race" and

I remembered what Hannah had told me. And another thing - I hated gym class and would have preferred to spend more time working on the school newspaper.

These directives came into force in a few short weeks. The new rules were swiftly applied, and my parents received the following note:

Dear Mr and Mrs Vogel,

The school is delighted to inform you that the female students will be transferred to the east wing of our building this week, following directives on education approved by the Third Reich.

All in the name of Germany and the German people!
Yours sincerely.

The Headmaster,
Herr Albert Müller.

Mutti did not seem thrilled by this letter, but my father was delighted. For him, single-sex education was a modern, progressive teaching system that benefited both boys and girls.

I was particularly put out by this change. Separating us stopped us from being friends. As I saw it, going to a mixed school was one of the few advantages over my old school in Wannsee.

So, one day at play time, I questioned Hannah.

"I don't understand why we've been separated. My grandmother says we are all equal. By splitting us up, aren't they treating us differently now?"

"Absolutely, Sophie. Remember when you told me about that girls-only camp? What I mean is, these measures will only make the country go backwards. It's like turning back the hands of time."

"Well, that doesn't seem particularly good for Germany. Could you speak to the headmaster and get him to change his mind?"

"My dear girl, my opinions don't really count at all. You know that I have Jewish blood. I fear that, like many other people, I will soon become an "undesirable" citizen here."

"Undesirable? What are you talking about?"

"I don't want to make you sad with these things Sophie."

"Have you done something wrong Hannah?"

"Nope. I've done nothing wrong. According to our Government, my only crime is my Jewish blood."

"And that makes you 'undesirable'? I don't get it."

"You see," she explained, "sometimes whoever is in charge uses their power incorrectly. Instead of supporting their people and listening to them, they make them bend to the government's own interests.

Sophie, I should warn you," said Hannah anxiously, "there are difficult times ahead..."

Right at that moment, the cawing of a pair of crows distracted us from our conversation. They were pecking through the garden refuse bin, and I watched them through the picture window. The scene chilled me to the core and gave me goosebumps. Thunder growled in the distance. In a flash, the sky lit up and we heard a roll of thunder followed by more. The rain that lashed the ground brought more lightning.

Hannah saw the fear in my eyes and reached out to hug me. I could feel her heart racing. Then I saw how sad she looked, out of character for her, wanting to tell me something that she could not put into words.

Lighting up the night

Sophie
Berlin, 1935

I consoled myself by writing to Omi to tell her how I felt now that Moshé was off-limits. Persecutions and prohibitions were multiplying by the day. Writing back to me, my grandmother encouraged me to trust that "sooner or later, things would go back to normal".

Time passed and fresh news arrived with the first snow fall.

It was a much colder night than normal and as I huddled down under the covers to read, a beam of light flashed in through my bedroom window. I sat up when I realised that this was no one-off.

Imagine my surprise when I saw my friend at the window of the building opposite, sending signals in Morse code using his torch. He looked much thinner than before.

My heart lurched but I pulled myself together and grinned at him. I raised my arms to greet him and then deciphered his messages:

"How are you?"

"I miss you"

"I'm sorry I've not been around."

"I'm afraid."

"They are coming for us."

I mimed that he should stay right there and dashed off to get my bedside light. On my return, I could send him my answers, in dots and dashes:

"I'm fine."
"I miss you too."
"You can count on me."
 "Hold on."

···___···___···____

His skilful answers flashed back:
 "Life in danger."
"Different this time."
"Sad."
 "We have to leave here."

···___·····____

······

And so on, our clandestine meetings continued through messages flashing from window to window, in the code that my own father had taught me. They were brief, fearful and full of questions.

Our fleeting words were like a meteorite shower crossing the sky.

Letter for Sophie

Moshé
Berlin, 1936

The clock struck five on a cold and rainy day in April 1936.

It had been a year since I'd last seen Sophie. At first, we'd met up practically every day. Then more time slipped away between visits, until the Nazi party approved the Nuremburg Laws in 1935, strictly forbidding us contact with Aryans.

A long time had gone by, and I missed chatting with my treasured friend. So, one morning, I decided to send her this letter:

Dear Sophie,

I'm writing to see how you're doing and tell you what I'm up to.

Since your mother sent Papa that warning note, things have got a lot worse. As you know, Berlin is not the city it once was, because of the rules made by Adolf Hitler and his men.

These absurd restrictions are making it hard for many families like ours to get by. Food is hard to come by. Today, for example, I had a lump of hard bread for breakfast, softened in milk. Meat and vegetables are luxuries for us right now. The worst thing is that many shops won't even sell us basics like food and clothes.

I have more free time now so I'm reading a lot. I'm obsessed with a book called "Metamorphosis" by Franz Kafka, who was also a Jew. I was up reading until late last night, and of course a nightmare woke me in the early hours with my heart racing! I actually thought I was Gregory Samsa, the main character in the book, and I had turned into an insect; I had a shell, and I was lying on my back unable to right myself.

It was a terrible feeling, Sophie!!

You'll be happy to know that I've begun to play more complicated pieces on the violin. Mama is helping me out with some Kreutzer studies, which has made a big difference to my technique. I love it and it makes the time fly by.

As for my parents, it makes me sad that they try to hide the situation and pretend like nothing's happening. We only go out when absolutely necessary because the SS could stop us at any time. You know who I mean, the Führer's soldiers, all dressed in black with a skull sewn on their caps. Remember my mother's eyes? They don't shine like they used to.

I can't go to the park with my friends any longer because they've put up posters saying that Jews are not allowed. We are systematically being shut out. Oh Sophie! I still don't understand why they hate us so much. What have we done?

Tata and Mama say that the Führer wants to portray a peaceful and tolerant image to the rest of the world by organising the summer Olympic Games, as people say that it'll bring a lot of athletes to Berlin.

The final straw was when they took my bike. How did the police know I had a bike? Let me tell you all about it...

One Saturday morning, two young men in uniform turned up at our house. Papa opened the door and they marched in without asking, right into the living room. Luna wouldn't stop barking when she saw them.

"Hand over your bike, runt!" one of them bellowed.

I made as though I hadn't heard him and kept quiet.

Papa lowered his head and spoke to me in a fearful voice.

"Do as the man says, son."

It was so unfair. So, I plucked up my courage and threw myself on the floor, dragging behind my bike, clinging firmly on to the back wheel and shouting,

"This is daylight robbery!"

My protests only made it worse. In retaliation for not being 'helpful,' they took Luna away in a muzzle.

I made a big mistake, Sophie. I've lost my dog because I was disobedient. What will happen to Luna? The days seem so long without her.

I'm sorry I only have sad things to tell you...

I miss you so much.

Moshé.

I crossed the road and delivered my letter to Adam, so that he could slip it to my friend.

Writing to Sophie helped me sleep better than night and it kept my hopes alive.

The Disappeared:

refers to a person whose whereabouts are unknown, without clarifying if they are dead or alive. There are usually political reasons behind forced disappearances.

My name is Josefina Expósito

Agaete - Gran Canaria

My name is Josefina Expósito Cabrera. I was born in Agaete, Gran Canaria. I have five brothers and sisters. Águeda, Auristela, Benedicto, Carmelina and Cristina. My mother's name is Juana, and my father was called César. I talk about him in the past tense because when I was very little, my life changed overnight - he was taken away and we were left with nothing. I've been wondering where he might be ever since.

A group of young men hammered on our door in the early hours, they grabbed Papa and took him prisoner. My Aunt Pino said it was because he refused to slaughter a sick cow, as he was worried about poisoning people, but he wasn't the only one taken that night. The Dawn Brigades picked up a lot of people. These squads of thugs were trained by people who had supported the Coup. Their task was to grab people from their homes and make them disappear.

Above all, my father was devoted to his work as the butcher in Agaete, which meant that many people knew and appreciated him. When he wasn't working, he went out picking watercress to make delicious soups and invited over all our neighbours who were feeling the pinch. The little time I managed to spend with him was enough to learn a few important life lessons - like how to be brave, stand up for the poor, love the land where I was born with all my heart, and he also taught me about the papagüevos, our island's name for the giant papier-mâché carnival figures with oversized heads.

"Josefina, do you see that black one? That's my favourite," he confessed to me one day, his eyes sparkling.

"Why that one and not any other, Papa?"

"You'll see, I started to work on it when I was very young, and I kept it secret until I could finish it. I wanted to surprise the whole village."

That was the first time I heard the word 'secret'. I didn't realise that this word would play an important part in my life after that dreadful night of 4 April 1937; just like the word 'fear'.

From the minute Papa disappeared, fear painted everything black. I often heard that we were "bad seeds that had to be weeded out." The adults did not let us go out, not even to play in the village square, unless someone went with us. So, I had no choice but to play tick, hide and seek and other games with my siblings and neighbours within our four walls.

When they took Papa away, I remember that a massive cloud appeared at dawn - even the old people said that they had never seen anything like it - thick and dark, almost touching the rooftops, hiding the endless sun in Agaete for days. It certainly didn't bode well.

As one bad thing leads to another, soon everything was out of bounds... even the most basic things. Hunger rampaged through so many homes on the island. Because of the food shortages, we were issued with ration books that - even after queuing for hours - only gave us the right to a few sweet potatoes, oil, chickpeas or sugar.

Nevertheless, thanks to hard work from my mother and a thin toasted corn gruel she made, my siblings and I did not go hungry. Some neighbours also fed us out of pity or to make them feel less guilty. There were seven mouths to feed at home and any help was always welcome.

I was a happy child until 1937, the year that Papa disappeared. After that, I had no choice but to see the world through different eyes, although some good memories do linger from that time. Like when I went with Mama and my sisters to wash our clothes in the stream at the Chorros Ravine, where gossip spread like wildfire. It was a source of good news, and bad, pouring over the ups and downs of love, about so and so and what's his name, telling stories, singing and playing. In that tiny corner of the world, we were happy and free. Nobody mentioned César Expósito there, or anyone else who had disappeared from Agaete, because talking about it touched a raw nerve.

We soon found out that these raids on innocent people had also taken place elsewhere on the island.

It is clear that Mama was, and still is, a woman with great inner strength, fortified like a castle. Thanks to her, we managed to get by in tough post-war Spain, relying on the black market - supplies and food that were sold

clandestinely - and the tomato harvest. We were short of everything back then, but my mother was ingenious and secretly sold our cattle's horns so that others could reuse them to make combs.

Despite these tough times, I still went to school in Agaete. Our teacher, Miss Dolores, called my sisters and I chatterboxes because we were never quiet in class, but I didn't mind... After my father was disappeared, I, Josefina Expósito Cabrera, took the decision to never keep quiet again.

POR VIA AEREA

13 FEB 37

LAS PALMAS

Coup d'Etat:

violent take-over of power over-throwing a legally- established government.

Fernando and Herminia

Josefina
Agaete - Gran Canaria, 1936

I'll always remember the day of the uprising, back on 18 July 1936.

So much hustle and bustle in the street at that time in the morning was out of the ordinary. I peered out through the bars protecting my window and saw a group of people armed with rifles heading for the square. One of them stopped right by my window, trying to light his cigarette, which forced the others behind him to slow down. They were talking about a Coup d'Etat in the capital, and someone called Franco. A few cars drove by, and people shouted "Viva España!".

On Saturday morning, Mama usually kneaded bread that she then baked in our oven using wood from Tamadaba. The smell of bread lured me out of bed that day. Just the thought of eating it with our quince jelly made my mouth water! Mama had promised us that she'd let us have a drop of El Valle coffee in our milk, although she didn't want us to get used to it. "Children shouldn't drink too much coffee; it's for grown-ups."

When I was about to go into the kitchen for breakfast with my siblings, we heard Papa and Mama talking,

"Juana, it looks really bad. A military group has revolted against the Government in Las Palmas de Gran Canaria."
"When did that happen, César?"

"Early this morning. Fernando told me that they practically got him out of bed to report it. A military coup against the Republic!"

"Mary Mother of God! But, who?"

"Darling, this is the work of a general called Francisco Franco who is here visiting Gran Canaria."

Mama crossed herself several times and whispered,

"What else did Fernando tell you?"

"He has taken measures to slow down the fascist troops to the north."

"Are you sure about this, César?" my mother asked.

"Don't worry, Fernando will know how to deal with it. I trust him entirely although not everyone agrees... particularly the toffs from El Valle."

"What are you insinuating?"

"You'll see, Juana, the rich will support the coup d'etat so they can keep on exploiting us."

As Papa and Mama were talking, I thought about how I liked dropping into Fernando's pharmacy in Calle de la Cruz to buy medicines that Don Victor prescribed in this surgery when we were sick. The handsome young pharmacist had caused quite a stir in the village when he moved to Agaete from Malaga, particularly among the women.

Aunt Pino told me that Fernando fell for Herminia at a carnival dance, in Santa María de Guía. Like every good Andalusian chap worth his salt, he never missed a dance.

Suddenly, Águeda sneezed one, two, three times. Our parents realised we were lurking nearby and fell quiet. We bustled into the kitchen, chorusing our 'good mornings'. None of my siblings asked about it over breakfast and we all enjoyed our bread and quince jelly together.

Fear in our Bones

Josefina
Agaete - Gran Canaria, 1936

The day after the uprising, Agaete woke up in chaos. Fernando, the pharmacist, had ordered the mayor to hold out and await reinforcements from the mainland. Unfortunately, they never came.

It was a Sunday, and my father took us to see "La Negra". He knew that we'd like that. What's more, he'd been working hard on her for weeks to bring her out to dance in our *fiestas*.

When it came to the Bajada de la Rama festival, which literally meant 'bringing down the branch', as crowds danced through the town waving palm branches, 'La Negra' was the kids' favourite papagüevo in Agaete. A rocket was let off to signal the start of the fiesta. We began at the top of the village, jumping around and dancing with a branch above our heads as the band played a pasodoble and several marches, and so we went on until we got to the Puerto de Las Nieves pass.

As we paraded through the square, we saw that they were handing out papers.

"Papa, what's that?" I asked curiously.
"They are pamphlets saying that the uprising has failed, Josefina."
"Up-what?"
"An uprising refers to people who want to impose their laws on society using violence."
"Aaaahhh, so it's good news, then," I sighed in relief.

"Yes, it's good news dear but we shouldn't let our guard down yet. Something tells me that this isn't over."

After a while, Papa asked my mother to take us home. When he came home that afternoon, he was subdued and seemed worried. He had been talking with Herminia and Fernando and he told Mama that things were not going well.

The next day, Monday 20 July, we didn't go to school because classes were cancelled. I stayed at home with my siblings that day, making giants and the big heads of the cabezudos out of papier mâché.

On Tuesday, almost at dawn, my bedroom floor began to shake. I got up and went to the living room. The lamp was wobbling, and I could hear explosions in the distance.

"Papi, what's going on?" I asked out loud but there was no answer.

I ran to search for my parents in their bedroom, but they weren't there. I dashed to the kitchen. Mama was glued to the radio.

"Good morning Mami, what's that noise? Why is the light shaking in the living room? And where's Papa?" I asked her.
"Good morning darling. It seems that a warship has been stationed out at sea for several days. It's setting off

its canons to scare us... even though we've hung up white sheets as a sign of peace. Your father has gone out with Fernando and a group of men, heading for Guía."

"But Mami, didn't we beat the coup?"

"No, Josefina, in the end, things haven't turned out as we hoped."

Papa came home later than usual that night. We huddled together in the living room, and he announced,

"It's not good news, I'm afraid. The Arcila coastguard bombed El Morro and we had to make a dash for it."

"Everything lost? What are you talking about father?" asked my elder sister, intensely.

"The warship managed to land its entire fascist troop at La Caleta and they are occupying the Sardina Port. The Town Councils in Guía, Gáldar and Agaete had to surrender in the end."

"Mary Mother of God!" exclaimed my mother.

Mama slumped against the wall to stop herself from falling.

Of course, nobody slept a wink in our house that night. Like a shadow, fear had even crept into our sleep.

Escape

Josefina
Agaete - Gran Canaria, 1936

Agaete could not hold out and it surrendered to the fascist troops.

"Juana, the town hall is in a right state. Some people are taking justice into their own hands and are retaliating against the fascist prisoners," said Aunt Pino rushing into the house as if she had seen a ghost.

"Don't scare me," exclaimed my mother. "Violence never solved anything."

After listening to my aunt, I was curious, and went out to see what was going on. At the street corner, I crouched behind the trunk of a palm tree. From there, I could see Fernando and Herminia trying to soothe a group of people.

"Of course, we must fight for our ideals urgently, but no blood should be shed!" shouted the pharmacist.

"The battle is lost!" exclaimed Herminia waving her pistol in the air.

"Please disperse! I've ordered for them to free the detainees," warned Fernando Egea.

Our neighbours were all on-edge, but unnecessary bloodshed was avoided thanks to this brave couple. Not a single person died in Agaete in the four days following the coup.

Later on, I saw Fernando and Herminia for the last time on 21 July, with our member of parliament Eduardo Suárez.

Whisperings in the village said they had fled because the Falange were after them. They intended to re-group the fight against fascism from the mainland.

According to Papa, they slipped out of Puerto de las Nieves at night in a longboat. Once out at sea, the captain told them that the propeller had broken and dropped them on a tiny beach close to Tasarte, on the west of the island, promising to come back and fetch them as soon as his boat had been repaired. He never returned for them.

The next morning, the Arcila appeared phantom-like on the beach, firing its canons pitilessly from the sea. They had sent the Falange and the navy to get them. It was a trap.

Seeing themselves surrounded, Fernando, Herminia and Eduardo decided to give themselves up, fully aware of their fate.

The news of their arrest spread like wildfire not only through Agaete, but also to the rest of the island.

They say that the night that they took shelter in the Cueva del Asno, Herminia revealed to Fernando that she was pregnant.

Dictatorship:

political regime that suppresses human rights and individual freedoms using force or violence.

Sima de Jinámar

Josefina
Agaete - Gran Canaria, 1937

My siblings and I usually played in our bedroom after dinner. After a while, we'd flop on to the bed, and were lulled to sleep by the chirping of the crickets.

The night they took my father, the street was deserted, and we'd been living in fear for a while.

Around one in the morning, three sharp raps woke my entire family. Our dog Catalina began to bark insistently, which was never a good sign.

"Don't answer the door, César!" exclaimed Mama. "They are coming for you. Quick! Escape via the rooftop, jump the wall and run to shelter in Tamadaba, no-one will find you there," begged my mother in her anguish. Her words jolted right through me, and I crept trembling into my big sister's bed.

"There's no point. I heard footsteps on the roof as well, they're everywhere! The best thing is to go and out and face these people," Papa answered firmly.

That was the last time we heard his voice.

Shortly afterwards, Mama took us to Aunt Pino's house to tell her what had happened.

As soon as her door opened, my mother fell into her arms, her eyes swimming in tears,

"Oh, Pino! They've taken César!"

"I know, dear Juana. I watched through a slit in the window how they took him into the Falange building. Bastards! I promise you that I tried to stop them, but they ignored me," assured my aunt, wiping her tears with her apron.

My siblings and I kept quiet, not fully understanding the nightmare we were living.

"Where is Papa now? Will he be back soon?" I asked, breaking the painful silence.

"Darling, we still don't know exactly where he is. But we'll find out and do all we can to see him as soon as possible."

For a time, we lived in hope that my father would walk back through the door any day, exactly where we'd seen him for the last time. Until someone told us that he'd been taken with others to the Sima de Jinámar... a volcanic crater!

I constantly wondered why they'd taken him there.

The Night of Broken Glass

Sophie
Berlin, 1938

The night of 9 November 1938, the Nazi monster was undeniably unleashed. That night will forever be etched on my memory. I don't remember the exact time, only that we heard loud bangs, crashes and shattering glass outside. Mutti and I ran out on to the street. Something terrible was happening.

"For the love of God! Have they lost their minds? They are smashing shop windows and burning our synagogues, cemeteries and schools! Even the hospitals!" shouted a young woman in despair.

A truly horrifying panorama lay before us: people were running around wildly, as if the very devil was on their tail; other stood stock still, staring wide-eyed in fascination at the sky thick with smoke; five young men in uniform spat at people and beat them up.

Against this dreadful backdrop, I caught sight of Moshé. I could barely believe it! He was just a few steps away from me! So much time had gone by... made only too obvious by his ravaged body - he was so thin that his clothes hung loosely around him. My heart skipped a beat and I screamed out his name,

"Moshéeeeeeee!!"

The pitch of my voice brought his gaze straight to mine. He flashed me a smile... although it was the saddest smile that I'd ever seen on someone so close.

"Let's cross quickly!" I begged Mutti, pulling her by the hand.

We stepped carefully, trying to avoid hurting ourselves on the shards of glass.

"What's going on? What's happening? Have they suddenly all gone mad? Have they destroyed your shop?" asked my trembling mother as soon as we reached the Abramsky family.

"I'm afraid so, Frau Vogel," replied a dispirited Josek, with a wary glance at the group of youths passing close by.

"It's not enough for them to mark us like beasts, but now they have to burn and destroy everything," said Moshé's mother shakily.

"Can you see that glow?" Josek pointed upwards. "It's flames. The synagogues are on fire, Anne!"

"What a disgrace! I'm so sorry," said Mutti, upset and on the point of tears.

Clara delved into her coat pocket for a handkerchief and held it out to my mother.

"Thank you, Mrs Abramsky. How can we help you?" Mutti asked wiping her tears.

"Get out of here, as soon as you can. It's dangerous for you to be seen with us," pleaded Josek.

While my mother said goodbye to the Abramskys, Moshé and I gave each other a huge hug. I got goosebumps as I felt his warm breath on my neck. I whispered in his ear,

"Sweet Moshé…"

And I felt his shy lips on the back of my neck.

"Thank you, dear Sophie," he stuttered in farewell.

I never imagined this moment would become so important in my life.

I suddenly felt Mutti pulling us apart.

"Let's go!" she exclaimed, tears still brimming in her eyes.

I kept my eyes on Moshé until I lost him among the crowd of men dressed in brown shirts, shouting "Get out, Jews!", "Bastard Jews!" These words stung and pierced my soul like a knife.

As soon as we crossed the threshold of our home, heartbroken, I cried to my mother,

"I'm so scared. What will happen to them now without their business? It's all they have…"
"I wish I knew Sophie! I just hope that this nightmare is over soon so that your friend and his parents can live in peace."

I slept in my mother's bed that night, and we held each other tight. I found it hard to drop off, as my mind ran through what was going on outside and worried about the Abramsky family. I wondered how Moshé must be feeling. And that stolen kiss also floated through my mind.

My feelings were interwoven with the burnt wood smell lingering over the skies of Berlin... The Night of Broken Glass.

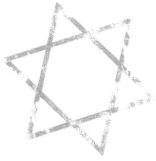

Letter for Irene

Sophie
Berlin, 1938

Dear Omi,

How are you? Today, I woke up sad.

Last night, we witnessed a living nightmare with our very own eyes. I don't know if you could see the Berlin skyline lit up with flames from your house.

Oh Omi! It was horrifying! Would you believe me that Friedrichstrasse was covered in broken glass? Mutti says that what happened is the greatest tragedy she has ever seen in her lifetime.

I was really scared. Unfortunately, the Abramsky's business was also wrecked. How will they make a living now? I want to help so I'm going to raid my piggy bank. Josek and Clara are always so good to me and treat me like one of the family. Moshé is so special to me, Omi.

What's happening in Germany? Why do people hate them so much?

I still haven't heard from Hannah. I wonder if she made it back to France, like she said in her letter. She was spot on when she predicted these terrible times!

The last time I saw her, her eyes were shining but not like Mutti when she smiles. I think that day she meant to say goodbye to us, although in the end something stopped her... She looked at me hard for a while, smiled and put her hands on her heart. Then she left the classroom and I never saw her again.

I asked after her a few days later and one of the teachers said, "That young woman is no longer teaching at this school."

Dear Omi, do you think that Hannah is all right? If only I had an address to write to her.

I'll ask Mutti if we can come and visit you soon.

I miss you.

Your loving granddaughter, Sophie.

A letter for my granddaughter

Sophie
Berlin, 1938

Dearest granddaughter,

Thank you for your letter and for expressing your feelings so clearly. Only brave, honest people can really open their heart like that.

I am so sorry that you had to experience something so dreadful, so monstrous... Even at my age, I can't begin to imagine it. The people governing this country have surely gone completely mad.

I'm sad I can't find the words to make you feel better. I must admit that I am both disgusted and ashamed.

Fortunately, there were no anti-Semitic events in my street, but the sky was ablaze. The news that has reached me is quite confusing; and there's an uncomfortable, heavy silence around every corner.

After reading your letter, I've decided to come and visit you both as soon as possible.

Sophie, I can only encourage you to keep supporting Moshé. I am so proud of your concern and affection. Knowing that you are nearby will be a comfort to him.

You know you can also count on me.

As for Hannah, it's so difficult to say goodbye without being able to express how you feel! You must cherish the times you had together.

We'll see each other soon dear girl. I'm sending you all my best wishes and hugs for both of you.

Your Omi, Irene.

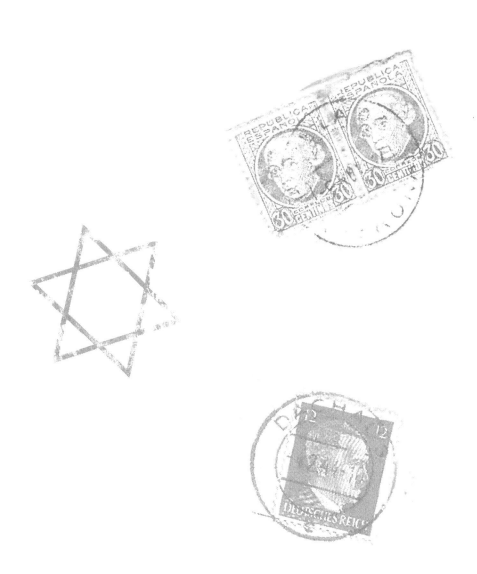

Thorns on Omi's white roses

Sophie
Berlin, 1939

After a terrifying night, the streets were plastered with thousands of prohibitions and from then on, everything just got worse.

Moshé's messages petered out and he seemed alarmingly thin. I began to lose my appetite and stopped meeting up with my school friends.

When I finished my homework, I took refuge in my room with a book. Lyman Frank Baum's characters: Dorothy Gale, the Scarecrow, the Tinman and the Cowardly Lion were my only company on those long, dark evenings. My parents realised that I was feeling down and one afternoon, Mutti appeared at the school gate. She wanted to surprise me, and took me directly to the Tiergarten, my favourite place in Berlin. She'd brought a delicious picnic of hot chocolate and pancakes with cranberries and raspberries.

"Darling, we've noticed how sad you are these days, you've even stopped meeting up with your school friends. If there's something bothering you, please talk to us."

To which I answered,

"Thanks, Mutti. I'm worried about the Abramsky family. They have been practically shut away for years, living under the increasing prohibitions and ever since, Moshé and I have been sending messages from our windows."

"I'm really sorry for them, my darling. It must be terrible to live like that, under surveillance and with so many restrictions. But what do you mean that you send messages from your windows?"

My mother listened closely as I gave her all the details. Then, with a serious face, she said,

"Sophie, I know that you care about Moshé but I don't like you hiding things. I suppose you didn't want your father to find out and thought it best to keep it from me."

That afternoon, Mutti managed to take my mind off things. We had all the time in the world just for us, playing hopscotch, elastics, hide and seek and tickle-fights. We had the best time and even lingered to watch the leaves falling from the old oak tree in the park.

As the weeks went by, Moshé's messages were increasingly brief and distressing:

"My mother is ill"
"We barely have anything left"

His words proved that the situation had got worse, as I feared. At that point, our communication was cut short, and I didn't hear another peep from him.

And one night, I heard my parents whispering in the passageway.

"As I walked round the city recently, I've seen the SS and the Gestapo entering buildings and causing a rumpus. From the street you can hear beatings, shouts and screams."

"The Government knows what is best for Germany, Anne. It's not right that those people keep on living here at our expense."

"How can you think like that? What's more, she really cares about Moshé," my mother said without thinking.

"What are you talking about?" asked my father, raising his voice.

"I gave Sophie my consent to continue seeing the Abramsky's son. Then all these prohibitions came in. Frank, whatever you think, that boy has always been there for our daughter."

"What? You mean to say that you both disobeyed my orders?"

"Look dear, that's not important right now," answered my mother, altering her tone of voice. "What matters is that the SS are dragging people like them out of their homes, never to be seen again. Where are they taking them?"

"Are you out of your mind? We are going to have a serious conversation about this when I get back from my trip. I'm going to bed, now is not the time to talk about this and I have to get up early tomorrow."

"Yes, we'll talk, but..."

"Shhh! I don't wish to discuss this," Vati overruled Mutti. "It's not our problem and if the Government has taken these measures, they will have their reasons."

Suddenly, the house fell silent. I got up, feeling that familiar lump in my throat. I could hear the incessant ticking of the cuckoo clock that we had bought on a trip to the Black Forest. I felt like my heart was going to explode. I walked with my arms held out as if I were sleepwalking in the darkness, so I didn't bump into the furniture. I went to the window that looked over the street, raised the glass and took a deep breath, while I tried to take in Mutti's words and erase Vati's dismissal: "It's not our problem and if the Government has taken these measures, they will have their reasons."

Furious, I went back to my bedroom. I tried to switch on my bedside light, but in doing so I knocked over a vase of white roses. I pricked myself on the thorns and a drop of blood bloomed on my finger. The pain stung like my father's words. Under my breath I murmured,

"Where are you, Moshé? What has happened to you, Hannah?"

I threw myself down on my bed and punched the pillow a few times, pressing my lips together hard. I couldn't sleep until gone midnight.

Fear was beginning to take over.

Save yourself

Moshé
Berlin, 1939

"The living room is freezing! Go on, run out to the backyard for some coal, let's see if we can manage to heat this house. At this rate, your mother will never get over her flu," snapped my father.

That winter was colder than usual, and our fuel store was running low.

"I can't do that Tata, I brought up the last sack of coal a few days ago."

"Moshé, we'll just have to start burning the furniture we brought over when we closed the store. The shelves and the counter will give us enough wood to keep going for a while."

Ever since our business had been destroyed on Kristallnacht, my family and I had been struggling to get by on very little.

"Son, I don't want to leave your mother on her own, she's still very weak, otherwise I'd come down to give you a hand. Remember to take the big axe to chop the wood properly so it can fit in the stove."

I opened an inner door from the hallway leading to the backyard. I got a real fright as I shone my torch through the tool shed. At the very back, an owl was watching my every move in the half-darkness. Nevertheless, the look in her eyes made me trust her and I felt like I could see the silhouette of Elwinga reflected in her pupils. Suddenly, I was overcome by a suffocating heat, my vision blurred, and I dropped to the floor.

When I came round, I realised that I was somewhere else. I had lost all sense of time. Somehow, I had got inside the hidey-hole where I used to play in summer. It was an extremely damp spot, that you could only get to through a metal trapdoor, half hidden behind a curtain. Despite my bewilderment, I got up and crawled out of my hiding place. I was surprised to spot a cigarette butt smouldering on the floor, a clear sign that someone had just been there.

I dashed into the house quickly and, finding the door ajar, I called for my parents but there was no reply. Everything was a mess, turned upside down. I felt a knot grow in my stomach and searched room by room, with no luck. I sobbed my heart out as my world came crashing down. Emptiness opened up before me like a gaping chasm.

From where I sat crying in the armchair, I spied a family picture of the three of us from back when we lived in Poland. I picked it up, kissed it and noticed my father's writing on the back. What I read made me fear for their lives.

Then I remembered Elwinga and I went looking for the little box where Tata kept my grandfather's pocket watch. I brought it out and held it tightly. Like a mantra, I chanted each of the words that the wise old lady had gifted me as I left the forest. Her message soothed my agitation little by little, but I had to tell Sophie straight away!

Outside, it was raining mercilessly. I crossed the road and hammered insistently on the door of my friend's building. Adam opened it with the same bitter expression on his face as the day I first met him, although his face lit up when he saw me.

"Moshé, have you gone completely crazy? What are you doing here? Don't you know how dangerous it is for you to be in the street at this hour? Come in! You'll catch pneumonia standing there!"

Adam told me that the SS had been picking up young people like me to work in the camps, and they had raided several districts of the city that night.

"I'm here about my parents... They've been taken," I shivered, with cold and fright.

Adam sighed and gave me a giant hug... the kind that might heal even your soul, murmuring,

"Your parents as well? A few hours ago, from here I could hear the unmistakeable racket of their trucks drawing up; the infernal shouting of those animals as they climbed the stairs, and the cries and pleading from those poor people they took away in the storm. I'm so sorry, Moshé."

Adam looked at me compassionately and he muttered,

"You should tell Sophie as soon as possible. Your friend's parents are away on a trip. She's upstairs with Irene."

I climbed the stairs two at a time and knocked on her door. Sophie opened up and with tears in my eyes, I told her and Irene what had happened.

Despite feeling devastated about my parents, and that painful knot in my stomach, I slept there that night knowing that I was protected, with no inkling of what would happen to me the next day.

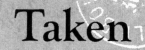

Taken

Sophie
Berlin, 1939

"I think someone's knocking at the door. Are you expecting anyone?" I asked Omi, glancing at the clock on the dining room table.

"Not as far as I know, particularly at this time of night," shrugged Irene.

The knocking came again, harder this time.

"Sophie, it's me!" I thought I recognised that voice.

My heart flipped and I opened the door in a flash.

"It's you, Moshé! You're soaked!" I exclaimed as I hugged him. "What's going on? Do your parents know that you're here?"

"They... they... they've been taken," stuttered my friend.

"Oh no! Say it's not true! Why them? Come on, come inside, and dry off. I'm here with Omi. Come and tell me everything."

"Well, I went out to get some wood, and I suddenly felt very hot - I must have fainted. When I came round, I went back inside, and everything was in a state...There was no sign of them. Half hidden in the mess of papers, I found this family portrait - on the back my father had written 'Dearest son, save yourself. We will always love you.'"

Moshé couldn't hold his tears back any longer and they came gushing out. I hugged him again, holding him close; I could feel the ragged beating of his broken heart. That's when Irene stepped in,

"Good evening. What's going on here?"

"Omi, something terrible has happened. It's Moshé's parents. They came for them."

"Are you sure, young man? Did you check the house from top to bottom? Might they have been hiding anywhere?" Irene interrogated him. Then, she stopped to think for a few minutes and turned back to him,

"It was the SS, wasn't it?"

"I'm almost certain, madame, they left everything a mess, like the time when they came for my bike and took Luna away. What's more, my father left this message."

Irene took the photo in her hands and looked at it closely.

"Bastards!" was all she could say.

She frowned, looked Moshé straight in the eyes and said calmly and firmly,

"I've always wanted to meet you but I'm so sorry that it's under these circumstances, my boy. You've been very brave to come here. You have nothing to fear from us," Omi looked at us. Then she fired instructions at me. "Come along my girl, our guest is freezing. We must do something about that straight away. Bring a towel and some of your father's pyjamas. Unless my eyes deceive me, they wear the same size. In the meantime, I'll run him a bath to warm him up. My mother always said that 'water refreshes our mind and clears our thoughts.'"

And with that, Irene disappeared down the hall. I asked Moshé to wait for me in the living room while I went to gather what we needed. He nodded, shivering as he thanked me.

I came back to find them chatting.

"You have to keep your chin up. We'll look after you from now on, until we can find out what's happening."

"Thank you madame. If only I knew where they'd taken them..."

"That's hard to know right now, seeing how things are. It's likely that they came looking for you and when you weren't there, they took your parents.

By the way, did anyone see you entering the building?" Irene had an air of Sherlock Holmes about her.

"I don't think so. I only spoke to Adam, but he doesn't seem to be someone who would tell, right?"

"That grumpy old man would take it to his grave. We've known each other a long time. You can trust him."

"That's a relief," sighed Moshé.

"Right now, you'd better spend the night here and tomorrow I'll take you to my house. Our first challenge will be to get to my district without you being noticed. Once we're there, we'll decide what to do. It's my duty to look after you. The streets of Berlin are teeming with of the Führer's men and women and riddled with informers."

"I don't know how I can ever thank you for all this. Your granddaughter has told me a lot about you."

"I am terribly ashamed of what is going on. This is the very least that Sophie and I can do for you and your family," said Irene, her head held low.

"I'll pack a bag so we can leave early tomorrow morning," I said to Omi.

"No, darling, you're going to stay put. The situation is tricky enough without putting you in danger as well. What's more, nobody can know that Moshé has been here with us, not even your mother, Sophie. At the end of the day, let's not forget that Frank works for the Government."

"OK. I understand. I will also take this to my grave," I replied sadly, knowing that in a few hours, we would be separated again.

"The two of us," said Irene, "will leave here a little before dawn and so we won't draw attention to ourselves."

"Thank you so much, both of you, I... I never meant to you to get into trouble on my account."

"Moshé, what is happening is not exactly your fault. The only people who are responsible are those who allow and support this crushing of human rights. It's my duty as a citizen to help you."

Omi looked at him with a tenderness that might penetrate your very core. Then she took him by the arm and led him to the bathroom. Seeing them like that, it was as if they'd known each other for ages although it was true in a way. He knew how important she was in my life, and I also talked constantly to Irene about our special friendship.

While Moshé took a bath, we made dinner. He said that he 'couldn't eat a thing' but Omi insisted that he kept his strength up.

After dinner, Irene left us on our own for a while to chat. However, he seemed miles away, staring at his family photo and its message. After a while, he came back to himself, looked hard at me, and asked,

"Sophie, do you honestly think I'll see my parents again? If I go into hiding and don't look for them, it feels like I'm abandoning them."

I really didn't know how to answer his question that night, where grief wafted not only between the walls of my home but through all three of our hearts. It goes without saying that the boy I met six years before had now become an adult.

Irene sent us off to bed at the stroke of midnight. That familiar knot was back in my throat. It was time to say goodbye. We gave each other a long hug as tears poured down our faces.

It was very clear that life was separating us again although now I knew that it would be different. So, from deep inside, I wished Moshé Abramsky the very best luck in the world.

I took my distress in search of my grandmother. She was waiting for me in my room with a copy of Wuthering Heights in her hands. On seeing me, she patted the mattress for me to lie by her side. Firstly, she kissed my forehead and then she whispered,

"Dear Sophie, I am sure that the two of you are also joined by an invisible thread. Never forget it. Trust in that special mutual affection you have for each other. Right now, no matter how much it hurts, you have to let him go."

Irene's words felt like a soothing balm on my soul. Suddenly, lightning flashed through the darkness.

Just as I was about to close my eyes, I asked,

"Do you think that Moshé will see his parents again soon?"

Irene sighed deeply before answering.

"I fear that Mr and Mrs Abramsky have completed their mission. This will be a very difficult lesson for him to learn. However, what lies ahead of him will give him inner strength, like when trees put down roots in the ground."

Although she was sad, Irene never failed to astound me with her wise words.

Just before switching off my bedside lamp, she said,
"My dear granddaughter, Moshé will soon learn to really see. I mean, see things with different eyes."
"Different eyes?"
"Yes, here," she answered, pointing to my heart.

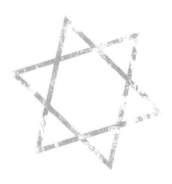

Too late

Moshé
Berlin, 1939

We rose at dawn. Irene had a shirt, coat and trousers ready for me, neatly turned up to fit. I remember the sharp, penetrating smell of mothballs.

"Moshé, it's time to go. This house is no longer safe for you."

I asked Irene permission to go into Sophie's room, I needed to say goodbye. She was still sleeping, and I tip-toed over to her - I didn't want to wake her. I kissed her soft, white cheek.

"Please, be on your guard now."

Before we left, Irene gave me instructions for our plan: "I'll leave the hallway first. Then, in the street, you must follow me at a safe distance so as not to arouse suspicion. Remember to sit at the front of the tram, so if an agent gets on, you'll be less conspicuous. I'll be at the back. I won't take my eyes off you. You'll have to count the stops: there are six to our first change. I'll get off one stop before you. Finally, when you get to Opera Square, get off and look for number 53. Have you got all of that?"

"Yes, ma'am. I hope I remember everything and don't make a mistake," I answered with my head bowed, des-perately trying to memorise everything she was drum-ming into me.

As planned, the tram arrived on time. I got on and sat next to the driver. After the first stop, two SS men got on. One of them struck up conversation with me.

"What a night!" he commented as he rubbed his hands. "Really, son, we need the rain, but not as much as this."

"You're right, sir," I replied without looking him in the eye.

"You seem like a good lad. How old are you?"

"I'm about to turn sixteen."

"Where are you from? Your accent isn't from round here, is it?"

All these questions were making my pulse race.

"I was born in Poland. I came to live here in Berlin a few years ago with my family. That's why I have an accent, sir."

"And where do you live exactly?"

"In the Mitte district, in Friedrichstrasse."

"Good grief! We've just been on a rat hunt round there, although the downpour ruined our fun."

His foul breath smelled of cigarettes and alcohol - it made my stomach turn and my legs begin to shake.

"We're getting rid of all that scum. Luckily, there aren't many of those bastards left round here," he looked at me again with blood-flecked eyes.

I almost threw up my dinner in anger. Later, a couple of stops before mine, the inspector got on. He asked for my ticket, and I put my hand in my pocket. I clumsily brought out the photo with Tata's note as well and it fell to the ground. Before I realised what I'd done, it was too late. The SS officer beside me bent down, picked up our portrait, looked at it carefully and read what was written on the back.

My fate was sealed.

The Vogel family trip

Sophie
Berlin, 1939

Things changed over the next few months: Vati travelled more and more often to Gran Canaria, working as a civil engineer for the German Government, and Mutti got sick. Her lungs were in a bad way, and we were really worried about her.

I had lost interest in Berlin for several reasons: Moshé and Hannah were no longer there, and school was just about following endless rules that were pointless in my opinion. I also spent long hours at home keeping Mutti company. The only good thing was that Omi came to visit quite often to care for her daughter.

As for my father, whenever he came back from the Canaries, I saw a change in him - he was happier and maybe more talkative than usual. It seemed like the island did him some good. He used to bring us back souvenirs and told us lively anecdotes and praised the beauty of the landscape, the peace and quiet and the friendly people.

One day, he left me speechless with his news:

"My girl, your mother's health is becoming quite delicate. On the one hand, her doctors have recommended leaving the cold, damp climate of Berlin for a warmer place. And on the other hand, the Ministry has told me that I must go to Gran Canaria for a long period of time. I must supervise various Government sites. Of course, both your mother and I considered you before making our final decision. We believe that a change won't affect your studies too much and it'll do you good, cheer you up."

"Sophie, darling," said my mother slowly, "given the circumstances, our only option is to go and live on the island."

I was so surprised that I couldn't utter a word for a moment, trying to gather my thoughts. Seeing me so quiet, Mutti asked,

"Is everything all right, darling?"

I pictured Irene and broke my silence.

"What will happen about Omi? She'll come with us, right?"

"I'm afraid not, Sophie. You know that she's lived here all her life and it'd be hard for her to leave her social life and her friends. Nevertheless, she's bound to visit us as soon as we're settled in."

Mutti carried on talking but my head was spinning like a top; I couldn't say no to this decision. First things first - it was her health that was at stake. Nor did I have anything to lose if I went... I wasn't particularly fond of Berlin and maybe the change would do me good.

"Vati, I have a few questions," I announced to break my silence again.

"Of course, Sophie, fire away."

"Do they speak German there?"

"No, Sophie. The Canary Islands belong to Spain, but as you pick up languages easily, I'm sure you'll learn Spanish quickly. Teresa, the Canary wife of a German colleague, has kindly offered to teach you and you two are bound to get along."

"I hope so, Vati. Another question: as well as Herr Kurt Hermann that you sometimes talk about, are there any more Germans living in Gran Canaria?"

"Yes, there has been a colony of Germans living there for a while."

"And do they approve of the Führer's ideas?"

"How can you say things like that, girl? Still going on about that?" he said as his voice grew steadily more intense. "I have explained this to you before. What's more, I am not fond of this rebellious streak, young lady."

His reply made me feel awkward and this time I said what I thought.

"Vati, my Jewish friends disappeared overnight. Hannah had to flee, and I've not heard anything more from her. I'm sorry that I lied to you, but you gave me no choice with Moshé - I loved spending time with him. And you know full well that he's been taken prisoner and I've not heard from him either."

I took a deep breath and steeled myself to keep on arguing,

"It's hard to stop thinking about those work camps that Omi told me about. How can I feel proud of belonging to a country which is so culturally developed and yet treats people like this?"

After getting all that off my chest, I fell quiet and waited for his reaction. He stared hard at me with his sky-blue eyes, giving a shine to his gaze that I didn't remember seeing before. Then he lowered his head and said,

"Sophie, whatever happens, you must know that I am proud of you. Right now, I can't give you any answers. Our government provides for this family and I trust the Führer completely. I warned you to stay away from that Moshé years ago because he was going to make you suffer but you disobeyed me."

Once he finished speaking, he spun around, grabbed his raincoat from the peg and headed for the front door. Before he left the house, I said in a clear voice,

"On second thoughts, I no longer wish to live in a country where people are hated, renounced and treated like criminals. I want to get away from here."

Vati stopped in his tracks and looked me long and hard in the eye. Then he left without saying goodbye, slamming the door behind him.

Mutti took my hands in hers.

"Sophie, darling, don't be so hard on him. Your father loves you very much. Sooner or later, he'll see things differently."

"Mutti, my father has not been the same since he began working for the Government. It's as if someone has covered his eyes and he doesn't even want to see."

The rain poured down on Berlin, battering against the windowpanes.

Goodbye to Berlin

Sophie
Berlin, 1939

After a few months getting ready to move to Gran Canaria, the time came to leave. Although I had got used to the idea and part of me was looking forward to it, deep down I had good reason not to want to leave my country. Firstly, it really bothered me that Irene would be staying in Germany, particularly in its current circumstances; second, by leaving, my chances of seeing Moshé again became even more remote. However, Mutti really needed to get better, and the island seemed to be her best option. The most important thing right now was her health.

Omi came to our house early that morning. My mother had told her not to come to the train station because she couldn't bear sad goodbyes, but Omi insisted, "Wild horses wouldn't stop me from seeing you off." That day, Irene wore her snow-white hair pulled back into a chignon, a long tartan skirt and matching plain woollen sweater. Around her graceful neck, she sported the pearl necklace that Mutti had given her for her sixtieth birthday. It was clear that, despite the passing of time, she was still an elegant woman.

"Please take very good care of Anne."

"Don't worry Omi. Mutti will get better when she's being cared for by that famous doctor and benefitting from the island's climate."

"I hope so, Sophie. I'll do what I can to come visit when you're all settled."

"I'd love that. What's more, my father says it's a wonderful place. If you come and see us, maybe you'll change your mind."

"My darling, despite being so far away, Gran Canaria seems to be a good option, particularly as Berlin is not the best place for your education right now. Germany is no longer a safe country."

"Omi, I'm scared that something bad might happen to you in this war that is looming."

"Don't worry, Sophie. I've always known how to look after myself. I'll be fine. You know I'm a tough old bird. What's important is that your mother gets better, and you are happy. You'll write to me, won't you? I'll be looking forward to your news."

"Yes, I'll write. As for me, I'll keep insisting and hopefully one day, you'll surprise us."

Irene smiled and stretched out her arms to hug me, like a bird spreading her wings. Then, she locked her emerald gaze on me.

"Can I ask you something?" I asked her.

"Of course. What is it?"

"Seeing as you know so many people, maybe you could find out where Moshé is."

"I didn't want to tell you anything without being entirely sure, Sophie. Although it's not much, I do have some news of him. Through a few trusted contacts, I worked out that he's been transferred to a ghetto. He's a strong young man, Sophie, and very smart. And he's got you in his heart which is bound to give him the strength to carry on. Be sure to keep the flame of hope alive. However, if I find out anything else, I'll let you know."

"Ohhh! If that's the case and he's in a ghetto, the news isn't so great, is it? But you're right, I will put my faith in Moshé's strength."

Omi Irene made me feel better and returned a glimmer of hope to me.

"One last thing - I told Adam that if a letter arrived addressed to me, he'd hand it to you in person when you stop by. I know that my correspondence will be safe with you, and you can warn me if you hear of anything."

When Vati came in to tell us that the official car from the Ministry would pick us up in fifteen minutes, Irene reached into her bag.

"Sophie, I'd like to give you our diary," she smiled.

"Our diary?" I asked in surprise.

"You'll see, it's all about us, the women in this small family. I started writing it when your mother was expecting you. There are some surprises in store for you. It's time you read it and I hope that it'll be a beautiful memory that stays with you, particularly when I am no longer around."

"Goodness Omi, that's such an amazing gift although don't say things like that!"

"I'm glad you like it, Sophie. It is the way of the world that we all have to go one day. I'd love you to keep this diary as a memory. Never forget our bond, our invisible thread. It's the best gift I can give you," she said placing the notebook in my hands.

"I can't wait to read it. I know! I'll read it on the boat crossing. I love you so much! You're one of a kind, thank you so much! I'll treasure it."

A sudden honking heralded the arrival of our car for the station.

"Right, enough soppiness, let's get going! Gran Canaria awaits you Sophie," announced Irene as she adjusted her skirt waistband.

"Yes, Omi, it does," I said, reaching for my bags.

Irene took the lead, and I paused for a moment on the landing. Something told me that I wouldn't be back in that house for a long time. I closed my eyes to remember the good times I'd had there. Curiously, the first thing that passed through my mind was Moshé, the day that he came to hand-deliver our letter. Before closing the main door, and as if someone inside could hear me, I said "Thank you" out loud.

My parents and Omi were waiting outside next to a large, black car as shiny as new patent shoes. For the first time in living memory, the three of them were chatting easily. Also, for the first time, I felt the excitement of starting out on an adventure.

As I bade farewell to the streets of Berlin from behind the car windows, I continued to turn over Irene's words in my head: "if I find out anything else, I'll let you know." She always kept her promises.

Francisco Franco:

Spanish dictator who took an active part in the Coup d'Etat on 18 July 1936. He was directly linked to repression during the Civil War and his dictatorship led to thousands of arrests.

The crossing

Sophie
Canary Islands, 1939

Several days of train travel brought us to Barcelona. My father made the most of the short stopover to meet some business contacts. A few hours later, we had set sail for the Canaries.

Fortunately, the sea was calm, and the boat's purser congratulated me,

"Sophie, the Atlantic is on your side. You're very lucky! It's not always like this. Sometimes, the beast awakens and makes the crossing a nightmare.

Manuel - Manu to his friends - was a wiry man. His skin had been tanned by the sun and he came from Laredo, Cantabria. He had wanted to be a sailor since he was very young because the sea was 'the love of his life.'

One afternoon, as we watched a group of dolphins playing, Manu - who spoke a little German - told me that he had taken part in the transfer of troops during the Spanish civil war:

"War is the greatest plague on humanity, Sophie. It is the worst of all evils, and it dishonours human beings."

After several days, as we approached the Canaries, we could make out the imposing figure of an enormous mountain that thrilled the passengers: "Is it a volcano? When did it last erupt? Can we climb to the top?" In almost perfect German, the captain informed us that it was the Teide volcano and then told us the legend of Guayota: the wicked creature that lived inside it a long time ago, who woke up Teide to spew its fire, lava and ash wherever it fancied.

The boat docked in Tenerife first for a brief stopover. Shortly after midnight, the ship set off again for Gran Canaria, the neighbouring island. I was restless and the thought of stepping on to dry land again kept me awake so I decided to get a breath of fresh air out on deck. Outside, I could only hear the noise of the engine and the sea breaking against the bow. I spotted Manu leaning on the handrail looking out to sea. When he saw me, he gave me a sideways look and raising his arm, he pointed to a light far away. It was white, flashing at irregular intervals and, when I counted, it gave three flashes for five seconds and the fourth, seven seconds later.

"What is it?" I asked, rubbing my eyes to wake up.
"It's a lighthouse, Sophie."
"Ohhh! I've never seen one before. Does that mean we'll be arriving soon?
"There are still around twenty-five nautical miles to go, the equivalent of forty-five kilometres. Look, the lighthouse indicates the far northeast tip of the island and guides us into port. Luck is with us because the night is clear and, as there's no haze, vision is pretty good."
"Haze?" I asked curiously.

He recited his answer like a lesson he'd repeated many times:

"It is a meteorological phenomenon formed by very small dust particles in the air."

"Ahh, does the lighthouse have a name?"

"It does," he answered as he snapped his fingers. "As it is on the Isleta peninsular, it goes by the same name."

"Wow! I'd love to visit it," I confessed enthusiastically.

"That's tricky. It's a military zone now and you can't go there. I've even heard that Franco has imprisoned people there just because they thought differently and…"

"Wait, did I hear you right? I interrupted him, amazed. "Do you mean to tell me that the same thing is happening here as in Germany? That there are also horrible places where they keep people prisoner?"

Manu held his tongue, as if he were thinking. He lit a cigarette and took a long drag. Little by little, small rings of smoke emerged from his mouth, like soap bubbles.

"Young lady," the purser drew closer to keep the conversation between the two of us, murmuring in my ear, "Hitler and Franco, Franco and Hitler are 'the same dogs wearing different collars'; in other words, while Spain is recovering from the war, Germany is preparing for a major conflict that will involve many countries.

I suddenly felt that knot in my stomach again. Sad, desperate images from the last few years in Berlin flashed through my mind. Why did my father never talk about this Civil War? I took the firm decision to hold my tongue and bide my time.

A greeting between colleagues

Sophie
Gran Canaria, 1939

The sun was peeping over the horizon for the last couple of miles as we sailed into the Puerto de la Luz. The island was finally in sight! Just before dawn on a day that promised to be hot and sunny. Although it was still early, the dock was bustling with life.

I hugged Manu goodbye. Thanks to his company and Omi's diary, the crossing had flown by. He blushed, reached into his pocket and presented me with a large seashell that I stowed in my luggage and still treasure to this day.

After disembarking, we saw a group of elegantly dressed men. One of them came swiftly up to Mutti, gesturing with his hands to make himself understood. She seemed to know what he was after and smiled at him.

He was tanned and very good looking, wearing a fine shirt, Sunday-smart trousers and a hat or "cachorro canario" as they called it on the island. He held out a small string instrument. My mother reached into her baggage for a pretty box of soap and offered it to him.

"Take it, Sophie, so you always remember this moment," said Mutti handing me the instrument. The first time that I came here with your father, I saw an old man play it right here, it was so enchanting and sweet... It's a typical instrument from the Canaries, called a Timple.

My hand caressed its bumps and curves, and I strummed its five strings... the sound immediately captivated me. Like magic, I thought I saw Moshé playing his violin just a few steps away. A sigh welled up from deep inside me. I missed him so much! I closed my eyes and felt the warmth of his presence.

I was brought back to reality by the horn of a green Mercedes, honking to get our attention. A well-dressed man got out of the car and made a beeline for us. He and my father greeted each other with a raised arm, just as he did with his workmates in Berlin.

"My dear colleague, I'm delighted to introduce you to my wife, Anne and my daughter, Sophie," announced my father ceremoniously.

"Welcome, I'm pleased to meet you. Frank has told me a lot about both of you. I am Friedrich Kurt Hermann, and I am here for anything you might need."

"Friedrich," said Vati, "as well as being German and an excellent friend, is a magnificent photographer and a person of considerable influence. We met the first time I came to the island."

"Pleased to meet you too. Yes, my husband has talked to us about you and how well you looked after him."

"It's the least I can do for someone that I consider a brother, Frau Vogel," he answered courteously.

"Forgive my curiosity, but what do you photograph, Herr Friedrich? What catches your eye?" asked my mother with great interest.

"I particularly like portraits. And if you like, tomorrow I can show you the studio where I work and take a splendid family portrait. Consider it my welcome gift."

"Oh! Thank you very much. That's very considerate of you," she answered, utterly charmed.

Then, Vati's colleague turned to me.

"Sophie, I suppose you'll be looking forward to taking a dip in the sea, right?"

"I'd love that. I even know how to swim."

"Really? That's fantastic! Well, we'll have to plan an excursion soon to the south of the island to visit its vast golden sandy beaches. I won't be able to go with you, because I'm always busy with party matters. However, I do know the perfect hosts."

"Really? When can we go?" I smiled at my father, opening my eyes wide.

"Darling, when the doctor prescribes sea-bathing, we'll be sure to go there."

"Can I ask you something, Herr Friedrich?"

"Of course, Sophie, fire away."

"Who are those men dressed so elegantly waiting on the dockside?"

"Ah, you're talking about the cambulloneros. You see, they are always here when a boat docks to exchange valuable items with the passengers and crew. By the way, that instrument you are carrying is popular in the Canaries. Would you like to learn to play it?"

"Thank you, sir. I would love that. What's more, music brings me happy memories of Berlin, and also Moshé."

"You seem very bright, you're bound to learn fast! Who might Moshé be?"

That was when my father stepped in,

"Come on Sophie, let's get in the car. Friedrich is a busy man and he's bound to have to get back to work. And your mother is tired. We have a lot to do now, and an appointment with the doctor bright and early."

"Don't worry Frank, I'm not in a hurry today. I am normally busy, although today, dear friend," he said patting my father's shoulder, "I've taken the rest of the day off to give you a proper welcome."

Vati nodded, and they smiled at each other.

"Of course," he said, looking at us before starting the car, "I hope you're hungry because I asked my cook Ursula to surprise us with one of her wonderful dishes. Today, we're having lunch at home, but I will give you a couple of hours to get settled in the hotel and have a rest. I'll be round to pick you up around half past one. Meanwhile, I'll do a little paperwork in Monte Lentiscal. I almost forgot! There will be six of us for lunch. I have invited the Jablonowskis, a charming couple. They know every inch of the island. It will be a most pleasant occasion."

"Thank you so much for the invitation," my mother added. "It sounds magnificent. We could certainly do with a little rest, particularly me. Thanks to my cough, I barely slept on the boat. Luckily Frank is a very deep sleeper..."

"Anne, I'm so sorry that you've not slept well. The humidity out at sea is dreadful. Don't worry, your health will improve immensely once our prestigious doctor starts treating you. The wonderful climate here will also speed your recovery."

"Herr Friedrich, where do you live?" I asked a little curiously.

"Right in the centre of the capital, in Triana, a beautiful neighbourhood as you'll soon discover."

Vati and Friedrich kept up their friendly patter during the car journey.

From the back seat, I couldn't drag my eyes away from the yellow sandy mountains and spindly trees, as tall as buildings, laden with small fruit. There was a strong salty smell. The sea was all around us and we began to get a feel for it. Mutti suddenly broke the silence to ask me,

"What do you think of the island, Sophie?"

"Ummm... It's a bit early to say but Manu, the purser, said that living on an island feels like the sea is constantly hugging you."

Mutti nodded and surprised me by saying. "Darling, during the trip, I couldn't get this poem by Goethe out of my head."

Fortunate Voyage

The mist is torn away,
The heavens turn bright,
And Aeolus unfastens
The bonds of fear.

There, the winds rustle,
The boatsman stirs.
Quickly! Quickly!
The waves rise up again.
The distant view draws close,
Land ho, I call!

"That's lovely! I didn't know you were a poetry fan."

She forced a smile, but the tiring journey was written all over her face. Even then, my mother still had that special glow in her eyes... a light that could eclipse even the moon.

As the car wound its way towards our hotel in Santa Brigida, the landscape turned a hopeful shade of green.

Same dogs, different collar

Sophie
Gran Canaria, 1939

Dear Omi,

"I miss you all the time. The news from Germany is disheartening. I hope that you are well, and that Berlin is still safe for you.

I was wondering if you had any news of Moshé. As for Hannah, I have to admit that so much time has gone by without word from her that I have lost hope of finding out what became of her. Nevertheless, my teacher will always hold a special place in my heart.

Anyway, here's my news.

After an extended stay at the lovely hotel in Santa Brigida, we've finally found a house with a big garden, full of flowers and plants! You can come and visit us now because our guest room is very comfy. You'll love where we live. It reminds me a bit of Wannsee, because the landscape is so green and there are always birds wheeling overhead making a racket. It's known as Monte Lentiscal. We were recommended to move there for Mutti's health. She's beginning to feel a bit better and no longer coughs so much at night. What's more, the doctor has said we should take her to a spa in Los Berrazales, in a town called Agaete, to the north of the island, where many people go to heal all their aches and pains. They say that the water flows straight from the depths of the Earth, giving it magnificent healing properties - people call it "miracle water". We'll head there in a few days so Mutti can make the most of it. I'll fill you in on all the details in my next letter.

We often meet up with Vati's German friends, plus their wives and children, and with Herr Friedrich Kurt Hermann who, I have been led to believe, is the head of the Nazi party on the island. Most of the children are younger than I am, and they go to a German school in the island's capital. The older children are not around because they go back to school in Germany after primary.

By the way, Teresa, the wife of one of Vati's friends, and a local here, has kindly offered to teach me the language; thanks to her, my Spanish is coming on in leaps and bounds. I'll short-ly be taking an entrance exam for a prestigious school called Las Palmas General and Technical Institute and if I pass, I'll start the next stage of my schooling there. Teresa told me that it was set up by Benito Pérez Galdós, an important writer from Gran Canaria.

She and I talk about all sorts of things, although I don't always agree with her. To give you an example, she thinks that Spain is faring much better under General Franco. However, someone that I met on the boat, I won't say his name in case this letter is intercepted, told me quite the opposite: Hitler and Franco, Franco and Hitler, are "the same dogs wearing different collars."

What's more, to give you a better idea, there are youth associations on the island called the Spanish Falange or the Female Section that are very similar to the Hitler Youth and the German Girls' League.

Dear Omi, I thought I'd left Nazi Germany behind when we moved here!

You'll be interested to know that we've been on a day trip inland. A couple who are friends with Friedrich, the Jablonowskis, kindly offered to take us to el Nublo, a beloved rock for the people of Gran Canaria with great symbolic value for them. Walter Óscar and Else Margaret own Electro Moderno, a busy, well-known shop in Triana, and they are always elegantly dressed in the latest fashion.

From the Summit, as the locals call this area, you get an incredible view that really takes your breath away. You can make out the shape of Gran Canaria with its deep ravines. It reminds me of a bicycle wheel cut into segments. As it was a clear day, not only could we see the sea of clouds - a very typical landscape on the island - but we also got a magnificent view of El Teide. It was majestic! Strangely, it was quite chilly, and we had to wrap up a little. I had a super time Omi, and the food was really tasty! We tried a dessert made out of almonds and eggs that was utterly delicious.

The Jablonowski have promised to take us to Maspalomas when the doctor allows Mutti to swim in the sea. They told us that the dunes there look like the actual desert. He is an excellent photographer, so I'll ask him to take a picture of the beach to send you.

We finished off the day with tea in the bar run by Adolfo-the-German, as people call him here. He is a very polite man with a beautiful convertible - he even gave us a spin round

El Monte. It was fun! He also plays the piano like a virtuoso and dedicated a piece to Mutti and me.

Don't put off your visit too long Omi and remember that I'm always eager for news of Moshé.

Lots of love, Sophie.

My friend Josefina

Sophie
Agaete - Gran Canaria, 1940

A few months after settling into our new home in El Monte, we went to the spa for Mutti to be treated with the medicinal water full of minerals, on her doctor's orders. As we turned on to the road to Agaete, a whole new landscape opened out before us. Not only was the north coast swathed in endless banana plantations and dotted with tiny beaches of black volcanic sand, but we also caught a glimpse of the other side of the Atlantic: wild, smashing into the cliffs and resounding off the rocks, although brimming with sea life. All of a sudden, with characteristic majesty, El Teide came back into view, a mountain floating surprisingly between two seas - the ocean and the sea of clouds.

"Oh! There it is!" I said, pointing to the mountain, as if seeing it for the first time.

"We'll go on a trip soon to get a closer look. Would you like that, Sophie?"

"Yes, I'd love that, Vati." Teresa told me that this huge volcano had been dormant for a while, but it could awaken at any moment.

As we approached Agaete, we passed a white-washed group of houses. Tiny flags were strung across the street. To our great surprise, the town was celebrating a very special day: la Bajada de La Rama. Crowds of people, young and old, danced and sang joyfully to the beat of drums. Most of them were carrying branches in their hands, waving them in time to the music. Later on, I found out that these branches were usually from pine, eucalyptus or pennyroyal trees. However, what really caught our eye were the enormous figures fashioned like people, with massive heads which seemed to be made of paper. They mingled randomly among the crowd as it swayed from side to side, hopping and jumping, dancing and constantly nodding along. Vati stopped the car and we got out. We watched from the pavement, fascinated by these characters with stick arms. Some of them menaced small children, bending right over them as the tots stared up in awe before scampering off in delight.

I got caught up in all the joy and the music. Without realising it, my legs were already moving in time to the catchy beat. I was overcome by an inexplicable happiness that I hadn't felt in a long while.

Suddenly, as a group of girls of around my age passed by, one of them caught my eye and smiled faintly; she waved to the rest of the group and came over to us.

"D'you want to come join the "papagüevas"?"

I smiled back at her and glanced at my parents.

"Of course, Sophie. Off you run!" Mutti encouraged me. Vati smiled and consented with a nod.

I grasped the hand of the girl who had invited me to join her group.

"My name is Josefina Expósito. What about you?"
"Sophie Vogel."

"Ah, I thought I didn't recognise you. You have a foreign accent. Where are you from?"

"I'm German, I've only been living on the island a little while."

"Your country is far away, isn't it? What brings you to Agaete?"

"It is. It was a long trip to get here. My mother is ill, and the doctor recommended that she came to live in a place with a warm climate. So that's why we've come to El Monte Lentiscal. German winters are long, and you can't imagine how cold it gets. Aside from that, my father works for the German government, and they offered him an important job on the island," I answered, almost having to shout over the noise.

"I've never seen them before," I said pointing to the giant figures crafted with oversized heads as we danced in a ring.

"Ha, ha, ha... You're talking about the papagüevos? See the one with the black face?" she said, gesturing upwards. "That is definitely my favourite."

Suddenly, the giant came over and danced near us, spinning round and round while Josefina and I laughed with glee.

"Tell me, why is it your favourite?"

At this very moment, the musicians began to play a *pasodoble* that set us all in motion again.

"I'll tell you all about it one day when we're on our own," she mumbled.

I shrugged my shoulders, wondering why she was so mysterious about it.

"Where did you learn to speak Spanish? You speak it well considering you're new here," Josefina inquired, raising her voice over the sound of the *fiesta*.

"When I arrived, I couldn't speak a word of Spanish, but I learned fast thanks to Teresa, a local lady. If you want, I can teach you a few words in German."

"Thank you, but it's best not. I've got enough on my plate learning to read and write. And when I'm not in school, I often go to work with my mother because my father was taken."

"What do you mean he was taken? Where?"

"I think," she said pointing across from us, "that your parents are looking for you, Sophie. If you're in the village tomorrow, come and play with me and my siblings. I'll tell Mamá to set the table for one more with the tummy rumbles."

"Tummy rumbles? Ha, ha, ha! What does that mean? I've never heard that expression."

Josefina laughed and took my left hand and put in on my stomach. "This is your tummy, I mean Sophie's tummy will be hungry tomorrow after playing," she winked at me.

"I'll see you in the village square at midday."

"OK, I'll be there. I'm looking forward to it! We're staying in El Valle tonight, but I'll ask my father for a lift to the village tomorrow."

"El Valle is one of my favourite spots, Sophie. My uncles grow oranges and vegetables there. Ah! Coffee as well. Mamá makes it when someone comes to visit and the smell of it wafts through the entire house. Sometimes, one of my aunts lets me take a sip. They say that the later you start drinking it, the better, because you get a taste for it and it's hard to quit."

"Well, I want to try it, Josefina! I'm looking forward to seeing everything you've told me about this place."

I held out my hand to her, but she surprised me by opening her arms wide for a hug. As she patted my back, she exclaimed,

"That's right, little Miss German. I'll see you at midday."

"See you tomorrow, Josefina. I'm so happy to have met you!" I answered enthusiastically.

"See you, Sophie. I think we're going to get along."

I went in search of my parents to give them a hug, I hadn't been so happy in a long time. One wish was burning inside me: if only I could tell Moshé about meeting Josefina one day soon!

Amazingly, my parents had got caught up in this throbbing energy from the papagüevos who spread joy far and wide from their great height.

The sky that day was as blue as the sea that hugged the whole coast.

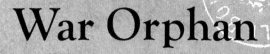

War Orphan

Sophie
Agaete - Gran Canaria, 1940

Josefina told me how tough it had been to lose her father. She had not forgotten him, and she never would. "It's like a splinter under my skin; it nags away at me from dawn 'til dusk," she always used to tell me.

Although nobody had explained his death to her, she knew that the night when "the dogs barked like never before and the crickets stopped singing," would be the last time that she ever saw César Expósito alive. Josefina had always been very intuitive, sensing things that other people couldn't see. She would have loved to have had the chance to say goodbye to him, tell him how much she loved him and douse him in the fragrance they made from Los Berrazales wild lavender that he loved so much to accompany on his final journey. But she was left wanting.

Her mother, Juana, was incapable of mourning him because she hoped that he would walk through the door one day.

In the blink of an eye, like so many other girls in Agaete, Josefina became a "war orphan".

"Do you know who took your father?" I asked her one afternoon when we were alone on her patio.
"The people on the right took him. That's why I do everything with my left hand."
"What did he do?"

"People say that he refused to sacrifice a sick cow so as not to poison the villagers. It's obvious my Papá did nothing wrong."

"I'm so sorry amiga!" I told her as I took her hand and squeezed it tight.

"Would it help if I told you I know what you're going through?"

"You? Really? Who did they take?"

"Moshé and his parents. Hannah as well."

"Were they family?"

"No, but it feels like they were. Moshé was my best friend and Hannah was my class teacher, the elder sister I never had. They both lived in Berlin and because they had Jewish blood, the Third Reich went after them. An anti-Semitic campaign began in Germany in 1933."

"Anti-what?"

"Anti-Semitic, it means against the Jews, people just like you and me but their religion is based on Judaism. My grandmother told me that millions of them have disappeared: kids, adults and old people. They've also taken homosexuals, gypsies and everyone who thought differently."

"Ohhh Sophie! That's... that's just terrible as well! And where are all these people now?"

"It is terrible Josefina, it really is. They live all packed together, surviving on next to nothing in ghettos or, even worse, work camps. I feel like my grandmother knows more about these places that she's letting on, but she's hiding it from me to keep me from worrying."

"Doesn't your father work for the German government? What does he say about it?"

"It's true. I'm sure that my father knows more than he is letting on, but he refuses to talk about it. Anyway, where do you think they took your father?"

"Papá was on a list with other people, Sophie. They were all taken prisoner, beaten up and then disappeared at the Sima de Jinámar where, people say, they toss the locals that they drag from their homes at night."

"That is dreadful! How can they? What can I do to help you?"

"Thank you, Sophie. You're already helping, just by listening to me. People in Agaete avoid talking about it. They're all afraid. This pain clings to us like a leach."

For a few minutes, we sat lost in our own thoughts. Then my friend broke the silence.

"Do you think that Moshé and Hannah might be in those work camps?"

"According to Omi, he could be in a ghetto, but by now, I just don't know. As for Hannah, I have no news and even though she promised to write when she got to Paris. That was a long while ago now, but I can only hope."

"That's the spirit, Sophie," answered Josefina flexing her fists, "I trust that one day we'll get my father's remains back."

Ausvitxia and Polania:

Play on words used by the authors in this book to recreate scenes from Auschwitz and Poland.

An underground kingdom

Moshé
Ausvitxia, 1941

I travelled here in a convoy from the ghetto where I had been held since being picked up on the tram. When the train stopped, we were all ordered to get off. The sign read "Berlin-Grunewald" station. Platform 17. This seemed to be where thousands of people were brought to be sorted into hundreds of trains.

On the platform, the Dark Green Ones (because of the colour of their clothes) - DGOs from now on - threw themselves upon us, beating us mindlessly.

"They're taking us to the Kingdom of the Beyond," a toothless old Starred One told me, with a far-away look in his eyes.

"What do you mean?" I asked him, stunned.

"Son, they're taking us to *Ausvitxia*. Loaded wagons like these set off there every day and always come back empty."

"*Ausvitxia*? I've never heard of it. Is it a city in Germany?"

"No boy, it's in Polania, an underground kingdom, the very furthest point from the Western world, the very ends of the Earth. That's where we're all going. It's like nowhere else," he assured me, opening his eyes very wide.

"A journey to the ends of the Earth?" I asked in disbelief.

"Actually, it will take you to the very deepest place you can go," he answered, pointing to the ground. "They need slaves. And that's us, we're going to work for them."

This didn't look good, but I wondered whether my parents might be in this kingdom, and I might find them there.

I slipped my right hand into my trouser pocket and touched Elwinga's watch. It was still with me.

A whistle blew. I raised my head. In the distance, a train was rolling in, pulling just fourteen single wagons for whole crowds of us.

"I don't know how they're going to fit us all in there. There's going to be a lot of shoving!" our protests mounted.

The old DGO locomotive puffed out a thick, white, intoxicating smoke from its great jaws. The steam seeped into the crowd and seemed to hypnotise fifty-seven Starred Ones into clambering on to the train in an orderly fashion, barely making a whimper.

I fully intended to return to Berlin one day, but no return tickets were issued, and when I asked a DGO, they frowned and answered,

"If you want to return, you'll have to earn it in *Ausvitxia*."

When the spell of this hypnotic white smoke wore off, we were already on our way to Polania on that rolling convoy that seemed in absolutely no hurry to get there.

The DGO locomotive was travelling at 370 metres per hour, the maximum speed that a giant tortoise could move on its endless journey.

The DGOs only gave us a bucket to use as a latrine and the smell was overpowering. Some people wanted to do their business outside the wagon, but we were sealed in from the outside.

Inside, we formed a hungry, thirsty human mess, although the worst part were the sleepless nights, really just one nightmare after another. There were so many of us squeezed in there that we had to take turns to rest.

Sometimes, once it had got dark, a boy visited us through the air grate. He beat his butterfly wings so fast and silently that, you'd barely spot him if you didn't watch closely. He would pour a milky liquid from his horn on to us that made pale spirals as it hit the air, smelling like Irene's rose bush. As these curls of smoke merged together, the stars closed in over our heads and we fell into a deep sleep. In one of those dreams, I was with Tata and Mama in our house in Poland; Saulo and Analía were waving frantically from the top of a hill at the *shabat* star while a voice whispered my parents' farewell to me. I woke up with a start.

Work makes us free

Moshé
Ausvitxia, 1941

The train slowed down in the thick of the night until it came to a complete halt. Five hundred Starred Ones had arrived at *Ausvitxia*.

I clambered on top of two suitcases and stretched as far as I could towards the air grate. The spectacle before my eyes took my breath away and I had to hold on tight to stop myself falling backwards. Stretching out before us, we saw a fortified enclosure, surrounded by wire fences and surveillance towers.

A deadly silence spread through our wagon, the first sign that we had been turned into silent beings during this journey.

Someone was rattling the lock on the outside. A DGO opened the door and received us with a dry bark of "Welcome to the world of everlasting darkness, you bastards." He let out a loud cackle. Not only did the earth shake but my legs wobbled of their own accord.

Another DGO bawled at us to get off the train and leave our luggage alongside. Tired and confused, we disembarked one by one. You could smell our fear from way off and those monsters knew exactly how to make their prey cower.

Not so far away, I could see small smoky grey trains standing waiting. "Looks like they are going to transfer us," I thought. Then, on a patch of open ground, the questions began: Job? Age? Healthy or sick? Depending on your answers, they sent you one way or another: towards the light or into the shadows, the end.

In the blink of an eye, healthy men and boys - who could work - found ourselves travelling on board one of those small trains. As for everyone else, we never heard of them again. After a while, we stopped in front of what I took for our final destination: the work camp.

The group of DGOs ordered us to get down from the grey train. Then they made us repeat over again, the message on a metal sign hanging over the gate, "Work Makes You Free." At that moment, I realised that if I wanted to go back one day, it would take a lot of hard graft.

The camp entrance was guarded by three enormous dogs with long, sharp teeth. Their eyes were bloodshot, and their bodies seemed to be lit by a supernatural glow. They were incredibly strong, and their job was to receive the new inmates and stop them escaping. After this initial checkpoint, we were bundled down endless steps, taking us deeper into the bowels of the earth.

I'll never forget that scene as hundreds of beings walked in formation, three by three. No longer Starred Ones, they had a new category, the Robotis: slave workers in the camp. Their faces spoke of gruelling exhaustion, and they wore a ragged striped uniform with a matching cap.

To us new arrivals, they reflected what we would quickly become.

Robotis:

Robot is a term that comes from the Czech word *robota*, that means servant or slave worker. It was used for the first time by the dramatist Karel Capek in his work *Rossum's Universal Robots*.

Robotis

Moshé
Ausvitxia, 1941

The sun was already rising as a few Robotis approached with brushes and razor blades. They had come to shave our heads.

Then they ordered us to strip and leave our belongings on the ground. With the deepest regret, I had to leave Elwinga's watch behind. I held it tight against my chest and swore I'd get it back one day.

From there, we went to the disinfection zone where we took a shower in a dreadfully hot, dark liquid that made me retch. The Robotis threw some rags on the ground, a cap and some wooden clogs for us to put on afterwards. Finally, we queued up in alphabetical order for the final touch: the "Welcome Protocol" that was, in short, stripping us of our name and our past lives. An expert tattooist, armed with a fine needle, etched a code on our skin - a series of numbers.

At the end of this whole procedure, we stumbled naked through the snow to our hut, where we put on our clogs and uniforms - decorated with inverted triangles.

The Roboti made us work like precise machines and perfect robots, performing tasks according to a series of programmed instructions.

The DGOs set the "Roboti programs" depending on the complexity of the work. These were simple or linear instructions when the task was not complex. We just needed to follow their orders to perform repetitive work. That was how they wore down our feelings totally or partially, also known as "Emotional Death". Consequently, just struggling to get by made us apathetic about suffering: the mechanism required to survive.

With problematic individuals, the DGOs used more complex programming, called "Structured Techniques". This was generally split into several mini programs with different sub-processes which gave them greater control, swiftly identifying troublemakers and so quashing rebellions.

We were also colour coded to show how we had ended up there: yellow for Jews, red for political prisoners, green for common criminals, blue for emigrants, purple for Jehovah's Witnesses, pink for homosexuals, brown for gypsies. Jews also had the star of David sewn on our uniform.

After the "Welcome Protocol", Bodo, an unscrupulous Roboti who worked for the ENSUCA — the Camp's Supreme Entity, run by the Great DGO, paid us a visit in our hut. He was our kapo, keeping his eye on us and enforcing tough rules. He waded straight in, beating us mercilessly... even then our hunger, thirst and fatigue were so strong that his beating could not hurt us, not even deep inside.

Afterwards, his bloodshot eyes locked on the Robotis:

"I'm going to read you the camp rules. From now on, the penalty for breaking these rules will be death.

1.   Here, you will be subject to the regime of the Third Reich.

2.   The right to happiness has been abolished.

3.   You are here to work and produce. There will be no free time, nor a fixed limit to how long you work.

4.   In *Ausvitxia*, obedience will be rewarded.

5.   Everything is systematically forbidden.

6.   Reason and conscience have no value.

7.   Any help provided to others will be repressed and sanctioned.

8.   In the camp, you will only be recognised by the number marked on your forearm. Your names and surnames no longer exist.

9.   The Great DGO will be watching day and night; any suspicious activity will be harshly punished.

10. Survival is just a matter of learning. From now on, the ENSUCA will decide who survives and who doesn't.

11. Opinions are forbidden.

12. Meetings are not allowed.

Once he finished, he turned on his heels and left the hut.

Sooner or later, these rules would quash my identity and end my existence. As time passed, I learnt to control my fears and, above all, attempt to find meaning in my life there. There was no way back from *Ausvitxia*, you just had to accept a whole new world.

Masterfully played by Rebeca Nuez Suárez, the work entitled Alone was written by the composer Laura Vega in 2014 as a meditation for solo violin, inviting the listener to enter a state of spiritual retreat. It is inspired by the text written by Pablo d'Ors:

"When the time comes, we are alone.
Looking into the void...
Sinking into the depths
Where wisdom beats
Listening to our inner silence..."

The violin

Moshé
Ausvitxia, 1942

Since arriving at the camp, I had spent endless days carrying heavy metal beams.

One day, something unexpected happened... It was December 1942 and Bodo appeared in our hut in his usual grumpy mood.

"Is there anyone in this disgusting dump that can play a musical instrument? We're expecting a very special guest at Christmas."

I didn't think twice and piped up,

"I can play the violin, sir."

Bodo swivelled his vast neck, and shot me a sharp glance, answering,

"Well, well... aren't you a clever Jew," flashing me his psychotic smile. "Personally, I can't stand that instrument. It sounds like a wailing cat!"

I looked him fearlessly in the eye. He stared back and warned me,

"You'd better be in tune if you don't want to be turned to dust, ha ha ha."

The next morning, I showed up bright and early at hut fifty-one. A DGO ordered me inside and gestured to the violin on the table in his office, ready for me to pick up.

The instrument looked old, but it was still in good shape. I turned it over and noticed the hump was carved in the shape of an owl. It immediately reminded me of wise old Elwinga. I wondered what had happened to her. Might she still be in the woods?

The bow was as light as a feather. I tightened it, rubbed it with resin and tuned the instrument. The official did not take his eyes off me and nodded his head, inviting me to play.

The music stopped the DGO in his tracks, gazing off into the distance behind me; he only pulled himself together when the piece finished.

He motioned for me to put the violin back on the table.

"Not bad, Jew. I want to see you at six thirty tomorrow evening in the officers' hall. I'll give you the right clothes for the occasion and you'll have an extra shower this week. We want to see a proper violinist, not a scarecrow!" he sneered.

The next afternoon, I turned up on time although a little nervous. The slightest mistake could cost me my life. I began my finger exercises to warm up before I went on stage, because the piercing cold really got to my

hands. When they called me in, I stepped up on the low podium being used as a stage. I closed my eyes and concentrated before beginning to play. I needed to immerse myself in the character of the piece I was going to play. I had decided that I would start my little concert with "Alone", my mother's favourite violin piece. Luckily, I played well, and it pleased them.

The violin, with its owl-shaped carving, seemed to have the same calming effect on anyone who listened to it - in this case, it calmed the savage beast. Once the show was over, they returned to their usual cruelty and heartlessness, stripping me of the instrument until the next time... because there would be a next time.

Whilst I played, this strange mesmerising effect and the sound of the violin spirited my heart far away from *Ausvitxia*. One time, I was with Elwinga, Saulo and Analía, in the forest. Another time, I was at home with Sophie and with my parents, which was the vision I went back to most often.

One afternoon, after I'd finished playing, I saw that two officers were whispering to each other as they watched me. The higher-ranking officer came over to me.

"What did your name used to be?"
"Moshé Abramsky, sir."
"Roboti, your hands work wonders on this violin. The DGO General Commander was delighted with your per-

formance at Christmas and has asked to see you perform here more often".

"Thank you," I replied politely.

"What's more, you seem clever and polite. We'll give you a test tomorrow to see how good you are with numbers. *Ausvitxia* is growing and we need an efficient office worker. For the time being, it'd be sad to wreck your precious hands by lugging sharp metal around."

I felt like a ray of light was shining into my life for the first time since I'd joined this underworld.

"Thank you, sir," I answered, not wanting to reveal my delight.

"It's getting late, Roboti. You should get back to your hut. Bodo doesn't take kindly to latecomers," the other officer warned me, glancing at his pocket watch.

My breath caught in my throat, and I had to do my level best not to show my astonishment. Fate had brought Elwinga's watch back into my life.

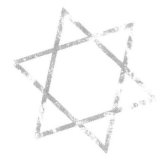

Smoke and ash

Moshé
Ausvitxia, 1943

I thought about Sophie all the time. I often fantasised that I could write her letters and it helped me feel connected to her and to life.

Another night, no moon no stars... like every night here so far. The camp is asleep. I'm making the most of it to write to you, and tell you how much I miss you, Sophie.

Very few of us are still alive from my convoy, the train that left platform 17 at dawn, one cold morning in December 1941.

I've managed to survive hunger and the feared selections. All the same, I'm so very tired. Every day, I tell myself - come on Moshé, chin up, this nightmare will soon be over. You're not alone.

I keep looking for clues to lead me to my parents.

I've seen a lot of people come and go. Some die in these harsh conditions. Others simply arrive and 'travel' straight to the beyond via the terrifying chimneys that constantly churn out smoke into the air from burnt bodies. This deadly ceremony is called 'The Transit'.

Sophie, I know I'm here for a reason. My mother said that every person is put on Earth with a mission. I think that my mission is to let the world know about this atrocity one day.

Herr Klimek and
the factory

Moshé
Ausvitxia, 1943

The ground was constantly shuddering with artillery strikes, a sure sign that the Red Army was on our doorstep.

For the last three years, I had been working in a sub-camp of *Ausvitxia* as assistant to Herr Klimek, a civilian who was working as the factory administrator. The plant made parts for cars and trucks such as drive-chains, crankshafts and various types of connecting rods and pistons made out of high-quality steel alloys for the top car makes in the world.

Herr Klimek was of German-Polish origin. He was shy and reserved, but still got things done. He was slow and methodical, taking his time to plan in meticulous detail. First impressions of him could be deceptive because he seemed cold, although he became friendlier as I worked closely with him, and gradually he began to trust me.

The day I went to work at the factory, Herr Klimek received me surprisingly formally, which seemed odd in *Ausvitxia*.

"Mr Moshé, this place could use a little housekeeping. We have a mighty task ahead of us and I can only do so much. Please do your best to make this office shine like a new pin."

It was strange to hear him speaking to me so politely.

"Don't worry Herr Klimek, I can do that," I answered politely, trying to sound like I knew what I was doing.

After a three-month trial period, Herr Klimek began to give me new responsibilities.

"Mr Moshé, as you are hard-working and well organised, I'd like you to give me a hand in more important tasks."
"Of course, Mr Klimek. How can I help you?"
"You're good with numbers, aren't you?"
"That I am, sir."
"Well then, please take care of the material we need for the order that came in yesterday. You must calculate the precise quantity of steel required so we don't have too much or too little. The DGOs are expecting the end to come soon, and they don't want the Russians or the Americans to be able to salvage anything here," he said arching his right eyebrow at me slightly.
"You can count on me, sir. I'm extremely good at calculations and I watched how you did it before."

The job was a success and meant that other car companies flocked to us like bees round a honeypot. As a result, over time, my list of tasks grew to exhausting limits. The good thing was that my mind was occupied for all ten or twelve hours of my working day.

This also included organising and filing the delivery notes and supervising machinery on the shop floor, keeping an eye out for possible production faults.

One day, when I got to work, the administrator took me to a quiet corner where no one could hear us.

"Tomorrow, we're expecting a visit from the sales director of a world-famous American car company. He's likely to put in an order for two thousand gearboxes. Do you realise what that means for this factory, Mr Moshé? So, your priority from now on will be to get this place shipshape and give the prestigious businessman the welcome he deserves."

"Don't worry, Herr Klimek, I'll have everything ready for him."

While I was working in the sub-camp, I saw a lot of representatives from European and American car makes. None of them was ever the slightest bit bothered that we were being used as slaves. At the end of the day, we worked endlessly until we could work no more. Some workers got sick and died for lack of care. Nobody mattered in the camp, there were always more Robotis to replace people who had passed away.

The soul

Moshé
Ausvitxia, 1944

In mid-December 1944, I went to the infirmary with a high fever, vomiting and diarrhoea. Dysentery was a bacterial infection that, along with typhus and scarlet fever, was killing us like flies in *Ausvitxia*.

My illness kept me in bed there for a while, exactly when we were bombed by the Allies. The brutal impact of the explosions made the factory a ghost building of twisted bones. Paradoxically, every bomb that fell brought me joy and a glimmer of hope that I might make it out of there alive.

I never heard from Herr Klimek again. He's bound to have closed the factory and taken his family back to Silesia. It seemed highly likely that those monstrous years were ending, and the Führer's men began to flee like headless chickens. They took swathes of Robotis with them, making them march through the snow, barefoot and barely clothed... on their way to the next life. I was still very weak. So, like all of us who could barely stand, they left us to our fate in the sub-camp. Why would they waste their bullets on the dying? Dysentery turned out to be the best thing that could have happened to me because many of my fellow inmates died on that infernal march, victims of the cold, hunger and thirst.

One day, the officer who had first picked me for the factory appeared in the infirmary with a case under his arm.

"Boy, before I leave this place, I'd like to give you this instrument. It will be no use to me where I'm going," he confessed.

The officer whipped out the owl-shaped violin and handed it to me, but not without adding,

"I have always loved collecting antique objects; it's a hobby I inherited from my father's family when we lived in Rhineland. I picked this up at an antiques auction in 1935. It was built by a famous 17th century luthier in the north of Italy. It's a priceless piece."

The officer pressed down one of its strings slowly.

"What's more, this violin has a unique soul... it was made using a very special technique."

"What do you mean, sir? A soul?" I said, pleasantly surprised.

"You didn't know about this, boy? I mean it, violins have a soul," the officer assured me.

"What do you mean?"

"You'll see, the soul is a tiny cylinder of spruce wood. It's a fundamental part that sends the vibration of the strings deep inside the instrument."

"I did not know that."

"Traditionally, for a violin to achieve perfection, both souls - the player and the instrument - must mutually possess each other. This is how a good violin ages: enriched with the soul of each violinist who has played it."

I couldn't believe my ears, and although I tried to express my thanks for this gift, I was too overwhelmed to string a sentence together.

"Keep it, it'll help you take your audience to another level."

With that, the officer put the violin back in its case, handed it to me and marched off into the mist.

Elwinga's wise words came back to me from the day she bid me farewell in the woods. A pleasant tickle ran through my body, and I swore that I would do my very best to get out of there alive.

Following the officer's visit, I began to gradually recover from my dysentery.

A few days later, I was awoken by the racket of the Red Army entering the camp. We were free! My camp mates and I hugged each other and wept a sea of tears.

Suddenly, nothing happened

Moshé
Berlin, 1945

I was convinced all this misfortune would end with our much longed-for liberation, but it did not turn out like that. On leaving the camp, we were faced with a long and torturous journey through Europe lasting several months. I finally made it to Berlin. The war had devastated the city, reducing it to dust and rubble.

I had just turned twenty-two and my top priority was to track down Tata and Mama. Despite what I had seen and lived through, I found it hard to imagine that they had been victims of the systematic extermination carried out by Adolf Hitler and his men. My heart also yearned for news of Sophie, so I set off on a rendezvous with my past.

I found it hard to find my way around this city that had changed so drastically. As I wandered around Berlin, I saw many groups of women clearing the rubble and sweeping the streets. Some of them were working inside the demolished buildings, passing bricks along an endless human chain. These bricks were then stacked neatly on the pavement to be reused.

My heart lurched as I turned into Friedrichstrasse. The scene was heart-breaking. With some difficulty, I scrambled up to what had been our home, burnt out and damaged by explosions. On the door frame at the entrance to our home, one memory from our past remained, our very essence... It was the mark of the mezuzá, reminding me of that long-ago Tuesday we moved in and how we celebrated the *janukat habait*.

As I stepped into my old room, I felt like I could make out Sophie's silhouette sending me messages from her window in Morse code. So, I closed my eyes and I sent two wishes out into the wind with all my heart. Then I looked down the street and made out the bent figure of a tall, skinny man... Adam!!

I jumped down as fast as I could and crossed the road. When he saw me, he was every bit as unwelcoming as the first time we met. He was the same grumpy door-man, but he had got so old...

"What brings you here, boy?" he spat in a hostile tone.

"It's Moshé. Moshé Abramsky" I answered, pointing to what was left of my building.

"What? Moshé? Sophie Vogel's pal? You're alive! I really thought you were a goner, boy!"

He came closer and laid his bony hands on my shoulders. He winked at me, just like he used to when he saw me. Then he wrapped his arms around me.

"It's a long story, Mr Adam. The Führer's men took me to an underground kingdom: *Ausvitxia*. A factory designed to annihilate thousands of people all at once, more than you can imagine."

"I know about it, son! It's amazing you are still alive today. I never liked Hitler. He always seemed like a dreadful fantasist," he assured me, furrowing his brow.

"How are you, sir?" I asked him.

"Mustn't grumble, Moshé. The war has destroyed all our lives. As soon as the bombing started, the street was practically deserted. The neighbours had to flee. Even then, I did not miss a single day's work. By some miracle, this building was not destroyed like so many others and keeping an eye on it has kept me busy. This absurd conflict has snatched away the people I loved most: my wife who died in an Allied attack and my only son who was called up, never to be seen again."

"I'm so sorry for your loss Adam."

"What about your parents? Any news?"

"No sir, unfortunately, I've not heard a peep since that dreadful day they were taken away. I've not stopped thinking about them all this time.

"What about Sophie?" I asked him anxiously.

"She's a real young lady now. The Vogels left six years ago to live in the Canary Islands. From time to time, Irene drops by and tells me the odd story about her family."

"The Canary Islands? That's a long way away!"

It was the last thing I expected to hear, not after I had come so far. It made me sad.

"They left because of Herr Vogel's work and Frau Vogel's delicate health. Although it would be best if you ask her grandmother directly, as she writes to her daughter and granddaughter all the time. Wait a minute..."

The old man bent down and picked up a chunk of brick. With a tiny pencil stub, he scribbled down Irene's address.

"Here you go," he said, stretching out his hand. "And three Marks for the trip. It won't be hard to find her house, she lives in the centre. They've reopened the train line from Berlin to her town."

"Thank you, Adam. I'm glad to know that Sophie and her family are safe. I hope we meet again."

"I hope so. Thanks, Moshé. It's made my day to see you again."

With that, I dashed off to the station and bought a ticket with the coins Adam had given me. I had to speak to the grandmother of my beloved friend and let her know that Moshé Abramsky was still alive.

As soon as I got to her town, it was easy to find Irene's house. I rang the bell and heard steps approaching the door.

From inside, I heard a woman's voice asking,

"Who is it?"

"It's Moshé, Irene. Do you remember me? I've come to say hello."

When she opened the door, she looked me up and down, hugged me and exclaimed,

"I knew it! I knew you were alive! I knew you'd find me sooner or later! I'm so sorry for what happened in the tram. I couldn't protect you in the end. But what really matters now is that you're here and you're alive."

We hugged each other for a while, without uttering another word. No words were needed.

"The first thing to do is get you a hot bath and a square meal. You're as skinny as a rake. I'll lend you some pyjamas and tomorrow we'll buy you some new clothes and shoes".

It's true, I was painfully thin, still getting over that bout of dysentery. My skin was a greenish yellow and I had huge bags under my eyes that made me look sick and scrawny.

Irene ran me a wonderfully hot bath and little by little I felt my muscles relax. Then I shaved and dressed in clean clothes. At the table, the old lady was waiting with beef stew and sauerkraut, the most delicious dish I'd ever tasted.

After a while, over coffee, Irene told me that Sophie and her parents had left for Gran Canaria because Frank had been commissioned with state business and Anne needed a change of climate for her lungs to recover. Once her son-in-law's job had finished there, they had decided to stay.

"How is Sophie?"

"She is thriving. She has adapted to living on the island and even has some new friends. You should know that she asks after you in all her letters, Moshé. She'll be so happy when I write and let her know you're back. All the same, she tells me that life in Spain is not so different from what we saw in Germany," explained Irene.

"But let's talk about you, son. Would you like to tell me where you've been all these years?"

"Irene, no matter how much I tell you, there are no words to explain what I've lived through. I have survived the most inhuman horror that anyone might imagine. I am exhausted and it's all so recent. It's hard to…"

"I understand, dear thing," the old lady interrupted. "Don't worry. It's a miracle that you got out alive."

"Although… there is one thing that I'd like to ask you that's been bothering me for a long time."

"Of course, Moshé, fire away."

"I don't want to offend you with this question. I've been wondering for a while if the Germans knew about the disappearances, the massive deportations and what was happening in the extermination camps."

"My dear boy, nothing here happened overnight. Before the war began, many people had already joined Nazi organisations which were spreading anti-Semitic hatred."

"But why did the rest of the population do nothing to stop it?"

"Hitler's machinery whipped up terror and fear that managed to keep society quiet. Many people looked the other way because it simply didn't affect them, they even made money out of it. And if you spoke out, they'd kill you straight away. Remember what happened in the tram? The terrible Gestapo held me at the police station. They accused me of helping a Jew. I'm only here today thanks to Frank's help and his contacts in the Government."

"But..." I interrupted her, "don't you think that other countries could have acted a long time before they actually did?"

Irene looked thoughtful for a couple of minutes, and then answered decisively,

"Of course. The Allies were well aware of the situation. My contacts told me that some Jewish organisations sent word of the exterminations to the American government. However, they were given the run-around and a bunch of excuses. I want you to know that you were always on my mind, and I tried to find out where you had ended up. I had promised my granddaughter. I felt partly responsible for you."

"When Tata and Mama were taken, you did everything possible to hide me, putting your own life in danger. Your conscience should be clear."

The old lady tapped the floor twice with her stick and bit her lip.

"How do you feel about staying here until you fully recover? Let me look after you, it's the least I can do. And that way, we'll have time to get to know each other and catch up on our news. I don't have any family in Berlin, and you are alone in the city, for the time being."

Chatting with Irene cheered me up. I took out my violin, my faithful travelling companion, and began to play a medley of popular Polish tunes.

It felt like life was just beginning again.

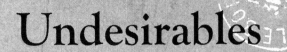

Undesirables

Moshé
Berlin, 1945

Irene was like a mother to me. Her care and attention helped me take great strides getting over my ordeal.

"Moshé, I'd be happier if my doctor August could give you a proper check-up. I'll call him and see if he can come over tomorrow."

The next day, the doctor came to the house and declared that I was severely anaemic, because I had barely recovered from the dysentery that had left me very weak.

"Irene, this young man needs to take antibiotics to cure this disease. I'm also going to prescribe him some vitamins to help his appetite. Try giving him lightly grilled liver. I recommend serving it with a little parsley and a squeeze of lemon, to make it taste better. We need to build up his strength because the antibiotics are pretty strong. And, before I forget, it would also be good for him to get some sun, for the vitamin D."

"Thank you, August. I am so grateful that you could come today. I know that you're very busy right now."

That very afternoon, Irene called her contacts to get her hands on the medicine the doctor had prescribed. In post-war Berlin, it felt like even oxygen was scarce.

Every morning, after breakfast, we took a walk along the river. These strolls with Irene were the best medicine to help me beat my anxiety and guilty feelings for having survived when so many others had died. She calmed my nerves, saying that this was normal among people who came home from the war, that I shouldn't worry, because it would get better.

Every day, like a ritual, we made lunch together when we got home from our walk. I helped out by peeling and chopping the vegetables while we listened to the radio.

Just a few weeks later, we heard on the news that the Allied Control Council - the provisional government - wanted to eradicate all trace of Nazi ideology in Germany.

This was doubtlessly the news we were all waiting for, drumming up a little faith and trust in governmental institutions. The crimes for these atrocities would not go unpunished, although the news also reported that some Nazis had fled the country, their whereabouts unknown.

It also reported that the German city of Nuremberg would shortly host the trials of the main Nazi leaders and, to streamline the process, an office for survivors who wished to tell their story would open in Berlin the next day.

I clapped my hands together in joy although as I jubilantly announced it to Irene, I saw that she was quiet, her head bowed. Her face betrayed her concern.

"Is something wrong?" I asked her.
"No, nothing Moshé, it's fine. But... don't you think you should work with the Allies? With all the

information you have, you could move mountains," she said, forcing a smile.

Almost a month had gone by since I got back, and I was feeling stronger. "Why not give it a go?" I mused.

"You're absolutely right, Irene. I'll go to the office tomorrow to tell them what I know."
"Moshé, there's something else. I personally promised that as soon as I had news of you, I'd tell my granddaughter. Would you like to write something to Sophie? I was going to send her a letter."
"I would really love that," I answered, smiling from ear to ear.

We got on enthusiastically with our letter-writing. I tucked some petals in the envelope, from the white roses that Irene grew, because I knew that Sophie loved them.

"Moshé, seeing as you are heading into the Mitte district tomorrow, could you post it from the central Post Office? That way, we'll make sure it gets to Gran Canaria as soon as possible."
"Of course, Irene."

Bright and early, I went to the Post Office and then on to the allied offices.

When I arrived, a secretary took my details. I found a seat and waited to be called.

When it was my turn, they ushered me into an office to meet an English soldier who spoke almost perfect German. His name was Andrew. By the stars on his uniform, I deduced that he was an officer - a lieutenant or a captain. Beside him, a secretary sat at her typewriter nimbly taking notes on our conversation.

After this first interview, I arranged to meet the officer again the next day. Andrew needed detailed information on the factory: names of business owners and officers who had worked together and this was all fresh in my mind.

I visited the Allied Control Council for seven days straight. The allied call for information was an unmitigated success and they were overrun. A few days later, the officer's assistant drove me to another spot to talk in peace, showing me into a meeting room with an oval table surrounded by chairs and an enormous wall map of Europe divided into zones.

"Wait here for the captain to arrive young man."

The officer's assistant left me on my own and I approached the map with interest.

Instinctively, my gaze turned to the continent of Africa and from there to the Canary Islands. I drew a little closer and saw that there were a few dots on the map that looked like islands. In English, someone had written: German Repatriation from the Canary Islands.

Sophie was currently living on one of these islands. We were so far away from each other!

Presently, Andrew arrived for our final interview. After a couple of hours, he announced,

"Moshé Abramsky, your help has been vitally important for us. We are most grateful. Tell me... how can we repay you for your time and effort, coming here to tell us all you know?"

"Thank you, Andrew, but I'm not interested in money. I just want to find out about my parents, where they were taken and if they are still alive. I'm sure that you can get access to the camp registration books. Their names are Josek and Clara Abramsky. They were taken away in February 1939."

"Fine, Moshé. I'll do what I can."

"Thank you, sir. Can I ask you something else?"

"Just say the word."

"Are you considering bringing Germans back from the Canary Islands?"

"What do you want to know exactly?" the officer answered, raising an eyebrow quizzically.

"By any chance, might you know Herr Frank Vogel? He and his family left in 1939 and they live there now. His daughter Sophie was my best friend in Berlin."

"You're obviously very observant and make good deductions. If you are asking, it's because you think that this man might have cooperated with the Nazi regime. Am I wrong? We actually began an interrogation process over there a short while ago with Germans classified as 'undesirable.'"

"Could you tell me anything else, please?"

"You're talking to the officer in charge of denazification in Spain. Naturally, we don't usually give this type of confidential information to just anyone, but as you are concerned about your friend, I can reliably tell you that Herr Vogel has been asked to come back to Germany without delay. He has been classified as an 'undesirable German'. Because he has been avoiding us, we have put in a request to the Spanish government to repatriate him."

After listening to the captain, my stomach clenched, and my legs began to tremble. I wondered what might happen to Sophie and Anne... How would they feel knowing that Frank was going to be put on trial?

Butterflies

Moshé
Berlin, 1945

Having said goodbye to Andrew, I went to stretch my legs and get my head together. It had been an intense week and I felt the weight of the world on my shoulders. I couldn't stop thinking about Anne and Sophie, wondering how they were taking all of this.

I changed course and headed off to Friedrichstrasse. I wanted to catch up with Adam because I hadn't seen him in a while.

I was surprised to see gangs of workers had already begun to rebuild the properties in the street where I had once lived. I looked for the old doorman but couldn't find him, so I dug out a scrap of paper and wrote him a note, saying that I'd been round to see him and that I'd come back another day.

Irene would already be making dinner and I wanted to be on time.

"Hi Moshé! How did it go today?"
"It was pretty good. I asked Andrew for information about my parents and he's going to do his best to find out what happened to them."

I went to wash my hands and noticed that Irene was studying me closely.

"Is there anything else you want to tell me, dear boy? You seem to be on a different planet."

"No, nothing. I'm just trying to deal with a wave of emotions. I'll get over it!"

As I came back, I was wondering whether to tell Irene what I'd found out about her son-in-law. I didn't want to ruin dinner or keep her awake at night, so I chose to save it for another time.

The next morning, after a delicious breakfast, Irene kindly offered to come with me to Mitte. She claimed she had business to do in town, but I think she wanted to keep me company when Andrew told me about my parents.

At 1 pm the Allied Control Council offices were hectic. We sat in a small waiting room until the officer appeared with a folder under his arm.

He smiled at me and gestured for us to follow him to the room where we had worked on my first day. Irene remained seated.

"Hello again, young man. Please sit down. I'll get straight to it."

He laid out the documents on the desk and announced.

"We've gone through the files from all the camps that were open when your parents were taken. The entry records state that they were both sent to the Sachsenhausen concentration camp, around thirty-seven kilometres north of Berlin. Their names and photos, from the front and side, appear in these documents."

I felt all the air leave my body. Closing my eyes for a moment, pain overwhelmed me, and I burst into tears.

Andrew paused so I could pull myself together.

"I'm so sorry, Moshé. Your parents were separated when they got to the camp and sent to do forced labour. It is highly likely that they died there."

Andrew got up, opened the door to call Irene in.

As soon as she saw the state of me, she threw her arms around me and whispered in my ear,

"I'm so sorry, darling. Josek and Clara will always be in your heart, I know they will. They wanted you to survive and you managed just that! Now your mission is to keep their memory alive alongside everyone else brutally murdered by fascism. Our history should be passed down so that this type of thing never happens again."

As usual, her words soothed me and she made me feel a little better, but even so, I could not get my parents out of my head. All that afternoon, I just lay on Irene's sofa, remembering all the good times I'd had with them and what I'd learnt from them. During the night, under the cover of darkness, I took up my violin again and played my mother's favourite tune - "Alone".

....

The next day at breakfast, Irene surprised me with her new plan.

"Moshé, do we have anything to gain from staying home and watching the rain pour down?"

"What are you talking about? Is it raining?"

"No! I just meant to say that there's no point staying here, surrounded by so many memories. I have a surprise for you. We're going to Gran Canaria! You can finally see Sophie again."

"Irene, don't joke like that, you'll get my hopes up!"

"I'm not joking Moshé," she said fishing the tickets out of her bag.

...

At 10 am on 10 September 1945, Irene and I left Bilbao, on course for the "Fortunate Isles". My heartbeat was once again strong and determined. My stomach was full of butterflies.

I know the truth

Sophie
Gran Canaria, 1945

Whenever I went to Agaete with Mutti, I dropped in on Josefina. We had quickly become fast friends. Like Hannah, she felt like the sister my parents couldn't give me, a real gift in my life.

El Valle became a very special place for my mother, who continued to take the 'medicinal water' there, and for me. When Vati travelled on family business - now his work with the Government was over, the two of us would head off to Los Berrazales for a few days. The glow of its sunrises and sunsets, visits to Tamadaba and its people had charmed us, and a little piece of our hearts now lived in this lovely place.

Going north always made us happy, like a celebration! Its rocky coastline, bathed in an intense green that tasted of bananas; its blue held the fragrance of the Atlantic and the grey-black of its rocks was a sight for sore eyes. There was always a new detail to spot in the landscape... The outline of El Teide, if there was no haze, could take your breath away, as could the high cliffs curled like the tail of a sleeping dragon. According to the Jablonowskis, that 'was just part of this beautiful although little known coastline.'

Omi wrote to us regularly to tell us all about the human injustices back home. We continued to press her to come and live in Gran Canaria where she would be safer. She brushed this off, saying, "I'll think about it. Maybe when you least expect it." Whenever we wrote,

Moshé's name would crop up, "Omi, have you found out anything?"

I often used to dream that one day, in one of those letters, she'd write, "Sophie, I have good news." This dream convinced me that I should keep on waiting and hoping... Sometimes, when Josefina and I talked about our losses, it made us sad but then my friend would take a good look at me and say, "One day I hope to be able to lay flowers on a proper grave for my father."

As soon as Mutti's health allowed it, we took the Jablonowskis up on their invitation and accompanied them on further excursions around this miniature continent. We often stopped off on these trips so that Oscar could snap this amazing landscape with his camera.

Although we enjoyed a happy life in Gran Canaria, many local people lived in real fear, like Josefina's family.

Until one day, our world was shaken to its very core...

It all started with a letter addressed to my father from the German Consulate in Madrid. I saw his demeanour change little by little as he read it.

"Anne, we must talk. It's what I feared might happen. Let's go out into the garden."

With my parents out of the way, I glanced quickly at the paper and froze, unable to react. Then, I pressed myself against the window and listened closely to their conversation.

"What's going on? What's this about, Frank?"

"Anne, remember the business trip I took to Madrid last month?"

"Of course I remember it."

"I wasn't entirely truthful with you. I didn't want to worry you. It wasn't a business trip. I had been asked to attend an interrogation."

"I still don't understand. What do you mean?"

"Darling, the Allies have me in their sights. They are investigating me. I don't know how to explain to them that I'm innocent."

"The Allies? What are they accusing you of?"

"They say that I am an 'undesirable German'. I have been reported as a member of the Nazi party and they are holding me responsible for building the concentration camps in Dachau and Sachsenhausen. They are also saying that I cooperated with General Franco on the defence programme, building bunkers and fighter batteries on the east coast of Gran Canaria. In other words, they are accusing me of working against British and American interests and they are requesting my repatriation. If that weren't enough, they wish to investigate me in Germany. If I go, it's highly likely that I will be put on trial and, seeing the state of play right now, that's not a good idea."

"But Frank! How could you have hidden all that from me? And now what? Where do you plan on going?"

"I'm so sorry, Anne. I only wanted to protect you and our daughter. We should leave here as soon as we can."

As my parents raised their voices, I began to put two and two together: his constant trips in Germany, our move to Gran Canaria, contacts with the Spanish Government, his business... Who was Frank Vogel really?

That night Mutti spoke to me alone. She looked tired and her eyes were lacklustre.

"Sophie, I have to give you some bad news. You're not going to like it and I'm not thrilled about it either. Vati is in trouble, so we must leave the island as soon as possible. I've been anguishing over this all afternoon."

"I can imagine... I read the letter that came today and then I heard you in the garden. I know the truth."

"I'm so sorry, Sophie. It's been a nasty surprise. We'll be leaving for Argentina in a few days."

"Argentina? We're not going back to Germany?"

"Sophie, a friend over there will protect your father and smooth things over. We have to forget about Germany for a long time."

"I understand. Is there nothing else we can do?"

"I'm afraid not. We will do this for the good of this family, to stay together. I've thought long and hard about it...We'll start packing tomorrow. You and I shall go to Calle Triana to buy what we need. It will be a long crossing."

"Mutti, I'll be very sad to leave Josefina. Can I at least say goodbye?"

"Of course you can. We will say farewell to our friends, but we won't make too much of a fuss. You never know..."

"What will happen now about Omi? She's bound to be worried when she finds out."

My mother hugged me and whispered in my ear:

"She is an extraordinary woman. I'm sure she'll respect our decision. I miss her sage advice so much at times like this, Sophie! I'll do my best to persuade her to come and live with us in Argentina. It's thousands of miles away, it'll be hard to live so far apart."

"I really hope she comes, Mutti! I miss her a lot as well."

Once again, life was testing us. What would this new country bring? Would I ever get to see Moshé again if I lived so far away?

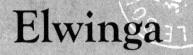

Elwinga

Sophie
Gran Canaria, 1945

The next day, we went shopping. The streets were busy in Triana, but before we ventured into the shops, we passed through Santa Ana Square to cool down by the fountain and so I could bid farewell to the cast iron dogs who looked like they were guarding the cathedral.

Later, as we strolled along, we loitered in front of a shop window, cluttered with antiques. Mutti wanted to buy something for Teresa as a farewell gift. I suddenly felt my heart in my mouth as I homed in on a tiny object. I lost all sense of time and tried to summon up the memory of the watch that Moshé had shown me one time, Elwinga's watch.

"Mutti, do... you... see that?" I mumbled, excitedly, squeezing her hand.

"What are you talking about?"

"The... the... the... watch."

"Sophie, please, you're scaring me. Are you feeling all right?"

"Moshé... is... here."

"Really? What on earth are you talking about? How can Moshé be here? All I can see is a pretty pocket watch in an antique shop window."

I couldn't take my eyes of it. I pressed my nose against the glass so I could look closer. Then I turned back to my mother and explained,

"That watch used to belong to Moshé. I'm sure of it. He showed it to me. His grandfather's initials are engraved on the lid, D.A., and his date of birth, 1868 (David Abramsky)."

"Sophie, if it's true then we should rejoice! Let's go inside and ask them about it!" said Mutti as she grabbed my arm.

We entered the antique shop on Calle Arena, and I rang a little bell that took me straight back to the Abramsky's shop. A woman's voice seemed to come from the storeroom.

"Please excuse me, I'll be with you in a few minutes."

I suddenly felt like someone was looking over my shoulder, vigilant of my every move. I spun around but it was just the two of us. My eyes came to rest on a painting. It looked like an old oil painting of an elderly woman with long, thick white hair. Like a bloodhound, I examined every inch of the mysterious portrait, painted in a remote, wild setting. An owl was perching on her right shoulder and one of her hands held a pocket watch.

"That painting has been here a long time, girl," commented a middle-aged lady as she emerged.
"Do you know who she might be?"
"Not the faintest idea. I don't even remember who brought it here because it was a long time ago and we get a lot of passing trade. The portrait dates back to the nineteenth century. That's all that's written on the back."

"The watch looks a lot like the pocket watch in your window!" I exclaimed pointing at the painting.

"Goodness! I have to admit I hadn't noticed that until now," she said, approaching the painting. "What a very observant young lady you are! Anyway, how can I help you?"

My mother stepped forward and explained our interest in the watch.

"Ahhh! Now I do remember that. It was brought in by a man of around fifty, elegantly dressed. He had a foreign accent. He told me that he was only here for a short time, and he was in a hurry, so it was easy to negotiate with him."

"Mutti, I have a big favour to ask," I begged. "Could you buy me the watch? It would make me so happy... At least I'd have something of Moshé's. It has great sentimental value for him."

"Of course, Sophie. I know how important Moshé is in your life. Consider it my gift."

I welled up as I touched it. I held it to my chest and hugged it close. No matter how faint, it could feel its gentle ticking.

Before leaving the shop, I turned back to the painting that had caught my attention. The old lady and the owl seemed to look deep inside me, as if they wanted to tell me something.

...

On 10 September 1945, at 5 pm, Vati, Mutti and I set sail from Puerto de la Luz heading for Argentina. I took some beautiful memories with me of an island that had stolen a piece of my heart. Josefina was waiting for me by the boat not only with her news - her unexpected departure for the Sahara - but also to give me one last massive farewell hug before I set off on another adventure.

Note from the authors

We wrote this book thinking about you. If a book like "Elwinga's Watch" falls into your hands, please hug it tight. It holds many hours of work and enthusiasm. If you've made it this far, we'd like to think that you enjoyed this story. We really hope so, it would make it all worthwhile. If you'd like to share your experience with us or you have any questions, please drop us a line at: alargalavidalij@gmail.com We'll get back to you as quickly as possible :)

Juanjo and Sandra

Thanks!

Thank you for taking the time to read
"Elwinga's Watch". If you liked the novel,
please review it on Amazon. You'll be helping
us to carry on writing stories for you. Your
support means a lot.

Juan José Monzón Gil was born in Telde, Gran Canaria. He is a Secondary School teacher, forerunner and coordinator of the classroom Timple Teaching Network. The short film "El Paseo" and feature film "La Sima del Olvido" are his most recent works on Historical Memory. "Elwinga's Watch" is his first book for young adults.
www.alargalavida.es

Sandra Franco Álvarez was born in Las Palmas de Gran Canaria. She loves novels and picture books. "Elwinga's Watch" is her tenth book for children or young adults. All her work revolves around nature, friendship, values and defence of human rights.
www.alargalavida.es

Index

150

POR VIA AEREA
13.FEb 37
LAS PALMAS

Manufactured by Amazon.ca
Bolton, ON

30711203R00157